'Move over

Alex sat up, clutching the sheet to her breasts. 'You can't sleep here!' The thought of his naked body under the same roof was nothing compared to the trauma of having it in the same bed, under the same covers. 'You have to get out of here,' she told him frantically.

'Look, you came here planning to sleep with me, didn't you? Well, that's what you're going to do... sleep with me!'

Dear Reader

Wouldn't it be wonderful to drop everything and jet off to Australia—the land of surf, sunshine, 'barbies' and, of course, the vast, untamed Outback? Mills & Boon contemporary romances offer you that very chance! Tender and exciting love stories by favourite Australian authors bring vividly to life the city, beach and bush, and introduce you to the most gorgeous heroes that Down Under has to offer...check out your local shops, or with our Readers' Service, for a trip of a lifetime!

The Editor

Deborah Davis was born to a quiet rural area and a mother who loved to read, and soon discovered the entertainment value of books for herself. An extended family of poets, story-tellers and lyricists made writing seem a natural course to follow.

Deborah enjoys watching romantic films, collecting family memorabilia, and eating chocolate—not necessarily in that order. She lives with her husband on a small wooded farm, where they raise Kentucky Mountain Saddle Horses.

BLOSSOMING LOVE

BY

DEBORAH DAVIS

MILLS & BOON LIMITED
ETON HOUSE   18-24 PARADISE ROAD
RICHMOND   SURREY   TW9 1SR

For my dad.

All the characters in this book have no existence outside the imagination of the Author, and have no relation whatsoever to anyone bearing the same name or names. They are not even distantly inspired by any individual known or unknown to the Author, and all the incidents are pure invention.

All Rights Reserved. The text of this publication or any part thereof may not be reproduced or transmitted in any form or by any means, electronic or mechanical, including photocopying, recording, storage in an information retrieval system, or otherwise, without the written permission of the publisher.

This book is sold subject to the condition that it shall not, by way of trade or otherwise, be lent, resold, hired out or otherwise circulated without the prior consent of the publisher in any form of binding or cover other than that in which it is published and without a similar condition including this condition being imposed on the subsequent purchaser.

First published in Great Britain 1992 by Mills & Boon Limited

© Deborah Davis 1992

*Australian copyright 1992
Philippine copyright 1992
This edition 1992*

ISBN 0 263 77577 1

*Set in Times Roman 10 on 11¼ pt.
01-9206-58057 C*

Made and printed in Great Britain

CHAPTER ONE

ALEX pressed the brake and gritted her teeth as she saw another hairpin curve ahead. She hadn't been able to relax her concentration for an instant since leaving the main road; there were too many dents in the metal guard rail to warn her what might happen if she did. The railing looked impossibly flimsy to her and below it the mountainside dropped away into a tangled ravine, so thick with vines and budding trees that no one would ever see her car if it went over. On her right there was nothing but sheer rock where the road had been cut through. She was starting to feel downright claustrophobic. Or agoraphobic. Maybe both.

And what did one call the phobia of meeting enormous logging trucks on skinny mountain roads? There might not be a name for that one, but its symptoms were very real. Halted breathing, white knuckles, a sharp pang of panic. Alex pressed the brake harder and moved her car as close to the rock wall as she thought possible. The truck driver still laid on his horn while his brakes screamed metallically. The logs were stacked high—huge logs held in place with thick chains—and Alex had a mental image of their breaking loose, crushing her little sports coupé into a silvery blue mess. Would she be able to leap free in time? And where would she leap to? Into the ravine, never to be seen again?

Somehow her car and the monster truck managed to pass. Alex expected a shower of blue sparks from the friction, yet they got by without actually touching—no side-view mirrors snapping off, not a scratch. She flung up a relieved look and encountered the truck driver's face. A pleasant-looking curly-haired man who wasn't feeling so pleasant at the moment. Alex suspected he'd just muttered 'women drivers', or something much worse. She was past him in a flash, but she appeased herself anyway by gritting back, 'Stupid road!' How did they expect people to drive here?

Another curve, and then without warning the road straightened out. Now this, Alex thought, is what one would call a picture-postcard view. Before her there stretched a mass of gently rolling hills dotted with grazing cattle and black fence-posts and varied brown squares of ploughed earth. She saw farmhouses and weathered grey barns with red roofs, and in the distance stood a little white church with a tall steeple. Then—as if to reassure her that she really hadn't driven a few decades backwards in time—there appeared a bright new convenience shop, and across from it sat an unpainted cement block building with a hand-lettered sign overhead proclaiming 'Jake's Garage'.

She had arrived.

Alex flicked on her right indicator and came to a complete stop at the junction before turning, using the time to unclench her fingers from the steering-wheel. What a harrowing drive! She wondered humourlessly whether Jake McGee sold tranquillisers at his garage as well as petrol and oil, and whether all first-time visitors to Conway County arrived feeling as if they needed them. This was about as deep into the sticks as she'd ever ventured... or should she say as *high* into the sticks? At least the county seat was situated on a nice tame plateau. Above the town she could see that there were more knobs and rocky-looking hill-tops, and then to her dismay she noticed tell-tale pathways cut through the trees for power lines. Where there was electricity, there were people, but who in his right mind would choose to dwell up there? She fervently hoped that the answer wasn't Tyson Conway.

She pulled her car alongside one of the petrol pumps and cut off the engine, and immediately a teenage boy loped over to help her. 'Fill 'er up?' The phrase was as customary for a service-station attendant as 'May I help you?' was for a sales assistant; he'd uttered it automatically. But when he leaned down to peer through her window he did a double-take and let out a barely audible wolf whistle under his breath, somehow managing to turn it into a 'Regular or unleaded?' at the last instant.

'Unleaded, please,' Alex said. There was a look that you developed when you were five-feet-one, blonde, female, and trying to succeed in the proverbial man's world, but she saw no reason to use it now. The boy fumbled a little as he inserted the pump nozzle into place, then he was back at her wound-down window, gazing at her with a shyly inane grin that she found rather endearing. He had a very nice face, tanned and healthy, framed by over-long brown hair that curled back along the edges of his billed cap. In spite of the generic blue overalls, she could see that he was wiry, strong and probably still growing. He looked to be about sixteen.

He also looked to be half paralysed. 'Could you check the oil?' She decided to help him out.

He leapt away from the door to the bonnet of her car almost before she'd released the catch. 'Yes, ma'am!'

Meanwhile Alex cast another look around the station. The front bay was basically clean and neat, but the side-yard looked like a car cemetery. She supposed all the junked vehicles were handy for spare parts... there had to be some reason for keeping them around. Most had been stripped to bare frames, and consequently a metal rack labelled 'Used Tyres' served as a kind of divider between the two areas. Opposite the junk yard several newer cars and trucks sat waiting to be repaired while a very muddy, very battered red jeep took pride of place on the racks. Alex could see overall-clad legs with heavy work boots protruding from under it. Jake? No one else was around.

'Oil's fine, ma'am.' The boy was back.

'Thanks,' Alex smiled, then added on impulse, 'and you don't have to call me ma'am. My name is Alex.'

She put out her hand and he hastily wiped his palm down a trouser leg before shaking it. 'John Shawn McGee. Pleased to meet you.'

'Pleased to meet you, John.'

'Better make it John Shawn.' His blue eyes crinkled appealingly. 'My daddy's a John, too, and it can get confusing. How did you come by a name like Alex?' he asked as she gently extricated her hand. 'Were your folks hoping for a boy?'

'No, it's short for Alexandra.' Her smile was purely automatic; she'd been hearing that joke all her life. Sometimes she produced a polite laugh; other times she just looked blank and said, 'What do you mean?' It all depended on her mood. Right now her mood was fine. She'd escaped that treacherous road with her life, hadn't she? She had escaped the magazine with her sanity, too. A temporary escape, of course, but maybe after the allotted four weeks she could go back a stronger person, ready to face the keyboard again, ready to meet expectations, heaven help her.

Lastly, but not leastly, she considered her mission to Conway County and still felt reasonably fine. Uncertain, yes, but also curious—as any journalist should have been—and sad, although more in a general way than a personal way. She hadn't *known* Tyson Conway, but it was sobering when anyone died as he had some weeks ago, with no family to sit by his bedside or to mourn him, and no one to inherit his property except a daughter who hadn't known of his existence until after the funeral.

Kate said he had wanted it that way. Kate McGee, his lawyer, had been openly distressed at her role. She'd sat in Alex's living-room last month and told her all the facts in an unwavering, quiet courtroom voice. But afterwards tears had stood in her eyes, making them as deeply blue as the Ming vase Alex had inherited from Grandmother Bannon, and Alex couldn't help seeing the irony in it all. Her father was dead, her *real* father. She hadn't known him. She couldn't cry for him. His lawyer felt more grief than his daughter did. Kate said he was a fine man. He had been loved by the community. He would be missed. Conventional murmurs that were heartfelt.

Alex remembered sitting there, watching Kate McGee dry her eyes with a tissue and regain her composure, and all *she* could think was that her life had been a lie. That she'd spent too much of it despairing over Robert, trying to make him love her, wondering why he couldn't love her, and suddenly, after years and years of pounding her head against that wall, a complete stranger had walked into her apartment and with a few words made everything clear.

Robert Stevens had not fathered her. She was merely excess baggage that had come with his marriage to her mother, a by-product of that disastrous first union to Tyson Conway. The adoption, then, could only have been a concession to Elise, for Robert was the most unlikely and uninvolved of fathers.

With the possible exception of Ty Conway.

Alex felt deeply disturbed by this whole affair. Why would a man remain anonymous to his only daughter until his death, then send a messenger to introduce him posthumously and to make known his final wishes? Why leave his property to her? According to Kate, he'd had an abundance of friends, people who had surely held more of his affection than she had... if she had held any at all, because she wasn't convinced that a man's love for a ten-month-old child could be nurtured and retained over a span of twenty-one years. Kate had tried to tell her that Tyson Conway had loved her, but Alex's strangled protest had cut clean through the attempt. She could believe that guilt had motivated her birth father, but not love. He wouldn't be the first man to re-think past life choices on his deathbed, she told herself. The idea of him loving her made her impatient and even a little scornful.

The lure of peace and quiet had brought her to hill country, not her birth father's final request. *But I am here, Ty.* She cast a brooding look towards the mountains ahead. *Providing you aren't too choosy about my reasons, you'll get what you wanted. I'll stay in your cabin. I'll see your country and meet your people. You'll have four weeks to make your point, whatever that may be, and then I'm free to sell everything you left me and walk away.*

But first she had to get the key and directions from Jake. Kate McGee resided in Conway County, but her position with the state attorney's office kept her in Frankfort all week, and, as she'd retained the key in order to supervise the cabin's maintenance, she'd had to do some quick thinking to accommodate Alex's impulsive trip. 'Suppose I phone my husband, tell him where to locate the key, and have him leave it at his brother's station...Jake's Garage? It's one of the first buildings you'll see when you reach town limits, and Jake can give you directions from there to the cabin.' Kate had hesitated, then the rueful smile in her voice had travelled clearly over the telephone line. 'And Alexandra, as one woman to another, I ought to warn you about my brother-in-law. When you meet Jake you'll think I've thrown you to a wolf... but he's really harmless, I promise.'

Alex remembered Kate's words now as she stared across at those two protruding legs. 'Is that Jake under the jeep?' she asked John Shawn.

The boy grinned. 'Yeah, that's him. And her name's Betsy.'

'Who?' Alex stared closer, but still saw only one pair of legs. He couldn't have a woman under there with him.

'The jeep,' John Shawn supplied, tongue-in-cheek. 'My daddy says she's the only lady Uncle Jake ever really loved.'

Alex peered at the miserable-looking vehicle. She thought she'd never seen so many dents or so much mud on any one object in her life. If that was the way Jake McGee took care of his ladies then no wonder his jeep headed the list.

'I need to speak with him.' She opened her car door and tried not to notice the way the teenager gulped over a glimpse of her legs. She was still wearing the suit she'd had on this morning, a lavender linen jacket with a matching straight skirt and white sleeveless sweater. It was from the new spring line at a shop she patronised; it cost too much, but looked good, and it was impossible to find business clothes that looked right on her petite frame without paying a premium price.

John Shawn followed her over to the jeep and, once they both stood beside the racks, squatted down to peer under them. 'There's a lady here to see you, Uncle Jake.'

Alex heard a grunt and then the sound of wheels rolling as Jake McGee set his mechanic's board in motion. Over six feet of male length appeared. Oh, great, another tall person! Alex thought resignedly. The man's blue overalls were darkly stained with grease; he smelled like an open can of Quaker State, but was obviously unconcerned with the fact. He got off the board, standing too close to her as he wiped his hands on an impossibly dirty rag. He held one of them out and Alex saw no choice but to take it. 'Jake McGee,' he introduced himself, 'and you, pretty lady, must be Alexandra Stevens.' The grin was pure male animalism... Kate had been right about that. In fact, it was just a little shy of being a leer. Dimples. The man had dimples. A deep one grooved into each cheek. He was very dark from the sun, his hair about three layers longer than his nephew's, the same rich brown colour, but straight as an Indian's. He had a rather prominent nose and high cheekbones. His black eyes glittered with devilment. 'What did I ever do for Kate to make her send me an angel like you?'

'You built your garage in a convenient spot,' Alex crisply supplied.

Jake McGee let his gaze roam over her with such unhurried thoroughness that in reaction she drew herself to full height... which wasn't much. 'You ever see hair so blonde, John Shawn?' he murmured appreciatively. 'It's almost white, it's so blonde!' His eyes locked with her large blue-grey ones, speculating over the frost he saw there. 'It's real, too,' he went on with authority. 'Know how to tell a real blonde?'

'I am not here to discuss my hair colour,' Alex cut him off dismissively. Her eyes were like ice; she only hoped that her cheeks weren't as warm as they felt.

'No, this is something the boy needs to know,' Jake McGee continued, unaffected by 'the look' which had squelched many more sophisticated advances. 'It's all in the scalp, John Shawn. See how pretty hers is? Pale, pale pink... like a baby's. You look at Adam some time, you'll see what I mean.'

Alex had no intention of asking who Adam might be. John Shawn was shifting from one foot to the other, half embarrassed, half admiring of his uncle's boldness. 'It's real nice hair,' he agreed, suppressing a grin.

'Yeah.' Jake's dark eyes narrowed consideringly. 'Of course, it's too short for my taste. A man likes enough to spread over the pillows.'

Short? Why, it almost touched her shoulders! *Pillows*? 'You're very familiar with strangers, Mr McGee.'

'Honey, I've been waiting for you all my life.' His teeth gleamed white to say he knew it was a bad line, but that he intended charming her with it anyway. Alex closed her eyes briefly, conveying a give-me-strength message, and when she opened them again his brilliant smile had dimmed a watt or two. 'Make it Jake.'

'I'd rather not.'

The grin, which he managed to maintain, had definitely taken on an edge now. 'You staying in town long?'

'I have no idea,' she lied blandly.

'Could get lonely,' the black eyes glittered, 'you being a stranger and all. Maybe I could find time to give you a tour of the county. There's not a lot to see...' he slanted a secret sidelong glance at John Shawn '...but I can show you a couple of out-of-the-way spots.'

The boy's smothered grin filled her in on the secret. 'Don't bother,' she dismissed the offer.

'You sure?' His deep voice went subtly rasping. 'There's nothing like a mountain road on a starry night.' A spark smouldered in the back of his eyes, and yet Alex got the impression that it was a practised look, a practised inflexion. That look, that tone, had probably sent dozens of country girls tumbling into his arms. She'd bet he carved big notches on his headboard. Or, more likely, his dashboard.

'Just you, me, and Betsy?' She allowed a hint of scorn into the retort. 'No, thanks.'

A faint red stained his high cheekbones to tell her she'd scored a hit. 'Better think about it,' he persisted stubbornly. 'No guarantee I'll ask again.'

'I hope not. I've run out of ways to say no.' She almost regretted saying that, but only because the put-down seemed to cause John Shawn more discomfort than his uncle, who was plainly an idol of sorts. On the other hand, Jake McGee deserved to be put down. If he wanted to show his nephew how to make a pick-up, and the thought of *that* cost her a shiver, then he'd have to choose another target. 'Mr McGee,' she sighed, 'do you or do you not have the key to my cabin?'

'You mean Ty's cabin?' His sudden gravity shocked her a little. 'Yeah, I've got it.'

'May I have it, please?'

'I can't help wondering what brings you up here after all this time.'

'What business is that of yours?'

'He was a friend of mine.' Jake's chin jutted out squarely. He was really quite handsome, with his lean tanned face. Even more jolting came the realisation that he had conveyed censure.

'He was my father,' she blurted defensively, and then wondered how, with a look, he had managed to make her feel this way... as if she had been at fault, as if she had *neglected* the man.

'Ty was your daddy?' John Shawn breathed. 'No kidding?'

'Apparently not.'

'Funny none of us ever met you. He never talked about y——' The boy broke off, colouring. 'What I mean is——'

'She knows what you mean.' Jake put a hand on his nephew's shoulder. His eyes were on Alex, though, and they were hard.

'I know what *you* mean, too, Mr McGee,' she told him flatly. 'And you know nothing about it.'

'I know that Ty had a daughter,' he challenged. 'A daughter who didn't show her face until he died and left her some property.'

'Where do you get your information?' Alex asked as witheringly as possible. A moment ago he had been coming on to her. Had her rejection triggered his contempt?

'I'm a few years older than you. Old enough to remember Ty and your mama when you were born.' His eyes narrowed. 'And, as far as the property goes, what happens at the court-house shows up in the newspaper. It's no secret.'

Then Kate hadn't compromised professional ethics and discussed her circumstances with the McGee family. That was a relief, although she wasn't sure why she should prefer being seen in a grasping light to the truth. Maybe because the truth was too painful to her yet. She didn't want anyone thinking 'poor Alex Stevens—had no idea she was adopted, had no idea her mother was married before, had to hear it from a lawyer'. Pretty pathetic stuff. Then she confounded herself by saying stiffly, 'I didn't know him.'

'Didn't want to know him, you mean?'

'No, that's not what I mean. Look, could you please just give me the key and the directions, and I'll be on my way? I doubt I could make you understand why I'm here, and, as I said before, it's no business of yours.'

'I guess you'll be selling out?'

The audacity of the man! She should have been freezing him with a look, but instead she was flushing guiltily and then hating herself for feeling guilty. How could she be expected to cherish a piece of land that had belonged to a stranger? How could she be expected to stay up here in the sticks? She was a city girl with a city career—providing she managed to salvage it. The country held little attraction. Conway County seemed like an alien planet. She didn't see how she was going to drive back down that mountain, but when her four weeks' leave was over, even if she had to charter a helicopter, yes, she was selling out. To Jake McGee she said evasively, 'I haven't seen the property yet. My key?'

He scowled and shoved a hand into a pocket, then abruptly brought it out again, keyless. 'I must have left it in the office. Hang on.'

He strode into the adjoining room and Alex hazarded a glance at John Shawn. The boy looked wary, as if he wasn't sure what opinion he held of her now. She regretted the fact that his uncle's animosity had affected him. Wanting to win him back, she aimed a smile and asked softly, 'Did you know him well?'

'Ty? Sure, we all did. He was a good man. He always had time for people——' he shrugged and Alex was touched by the emotion in his eyes—'especially kids. He taught me how to whittle when I was about ten. We carved this little basket out of a peach seed.'

'I'd love to see it.'

He looked startled. 'I reckon it's around the house somewhere. My mom keeps everything. You want to see some real carving, though, you go visit my Grandma McGee. She's got a whole cabinet full of Ty's stuff.'

Jake was back, dropping a key into her palm. 'OK,' he said briskly, as if he couldn't wait to see the back of her now, 'you stay on this main road about two miles until you pass the auction barn, then take the second right. That road winds up about a mile and——'

'Up?' Alex grimaced.

'Yeah, Ty's cabin sits about halfway up that hill,' he pointed to a spot in the distance, 'a mile and three-quarters after you turn. Watch your milometer,' he suggested drily. 'You won't see many houses up that way. Just look for a log cabin with cedar shakes on the roof.'

John Shawn seemed to be waiting for something. He looked at his uncle uncertainly, finally adding, 'Ty's cabin is——'

'About the prettiest one up there,' Jake cut out the boy's voice. 'You can't miss it.' A bell rang and he jerked his head towards the ancient flatbed truck that had pulled on to the yard. 'Looks as if George is here for his Friday fill-up.' John Shawn stood where he was, a faintly disturbed air about him, and Jake urged impatiently, 'Get a move on, son.'

'Uncle Jake, I don't think——'

'Am I paying you to think or to pump gas?'

His mouth open to argue, the teenager shrugged instead. 'See you around, Alex.'

'I hope so.' She watched him lope off, then frowned at his uncle. 'Are you always so bossy with him?'

'He's used to it,' he drawled, and Alex discerned that it was more a needle for her than a statement of fact. 'That will be twelve-fifty, ma'am.'

'Pardon me?'

'For the fill-up.' Her blush told him that she had completely forgotten. He produced another hateful grin. 'I can't stay in business giving it away.'

And I can't stay in town long if there are any more men like you, Alex was thinking sourly a few minutes later. She'd driven as far as the small modern supermarket and was filling her trolley with a few essentials. Eggs, bread, milk, coffee, salad, juice, and on impulse two glossy magazines from the check-out display. What was she going to do up here for four weeks? Prudently she added another magazine to the conveyor belt. A plump brunette in a blue smock rang her purchases through. 'Are you new in town, hon?'

Alex glanced up from her wallet. 'Yes, I am.'

'I knew it! You wouldn't be buyin' groceries if you were just passin' through.' The woman whipped out a paper bag. 'You plan on stayin' long?'

'A few weeks.' Alex tore a traveller's cheque from her booklet.

'Do you have folks here?'

'No.' She handed over the cheque. Not any more.

'Friends, then,' the lady guessed pleasantly. 'A girl like you must have lots of friends.'

Alex had no answer for that.

Giving up, the cashier finished her sale in silence. But, as Alex wheeled her purchases to the car afterwards, she felt a twinge of regret for her reticence. It was pretty hypocritical, considering she asked people questions for a living.

She located the auction barn and turned right as she had been told. She found the road leading up the mountainside to be poorly paved and pot-holed. The edges of the tarmac were crumbling in places and, like the potholes, had been patched with gravel. Alex had no trouble deducing why. The sparse population meant sparse votes, which in turn meant that the road wasn't a priority on the county's list for maintenance. Even in a town as tiny as this, politics ruled.

The road verges had been mowed, at least, and beyond them an abundance of trees decorated the banks with white blossom. There was no cut-away rock face here, just woods on either side, the tender buds of new leaves contrasting with a ground cover of dead leaves and twigs and brown pine needles. She passed a shack that looked abandoned, then an aging mobile home with red gingham curtains at the windows, and later a little frame house with a sagging front porch. There was about half a mile between dwellings to tell her that these people valued some space around them, which suited her just fine. She wasn't planning any social calls. She just wanted to relax and think and—this came out of the blue—reach a decision.

That shook her, thrown in by her subconscious when she hadn't expected it. Frowning as she negotiated a snaking curve, she asked herself, What decision? Her job? And what was she going to do? Acknowledge that she hated every minute of it, resign, and look for a position elsewhere? Not likely, when the magazine had been in the family for nearly a century—her mother's family, not Robert's. But during his brief reign as editor he had made her life such hell that she still felt repercussions— like a legacy of self-doubt.

Yet whenever leaving crossed her mind she thought of Grandfather Bannon with his big white moustache, sitting behind the massive editor's desk, enthralling her with those stories. His first interview and all the ones that had followed. He'd expected Alex to carry on the tradition, and she loved to write, so what was the problem? Memories of Robert, methodically tearing apart every assignment she completed? Or maybe he had been right. Maybe she *was* short on talent.

Give it a *rest*, she implored her persistent brain. That must be the cabin up ahead. It seemed charming, made of thick logs with a peaked, cedar-shingled roof and a porch that wrapped around the front and both sides, nestled back in the trees with only a minimum of kept lawn. Alex pulled the car into the drive and parked it, then sat thoughtfully chewing her lip. For some reason the property was a complete mismatch to her expectations. She tried to remember exactly how Kate had described it, but couldn't recall any adjectives other than 'small' and 'fairly secluded', which certainly applied here. She'd followed Jake McGee's directions implicitly. This had to be the place, she decided, but still couldn't bring herself to get out of the car. Walking inside was going to make him real. She'd kept Tyson Conway a cardboard figure for weeks, but stepping inside his house would be like breathing life into him, acknowledging her link with him, facing her mother's doomed first marriage. Dealing with the truth.

After a moment she swallowed down the panic and began gathering up her things. Just the groceries and her vanity case for now—the rest could wait. She might not be able to stay. She might not want to stay. She hadn't counted on feeling so eerie about this... as if she were trespassing, or, as Jake McGee had implied, capitalising on the main chance. Alex hated the fact that she was so vulnerable as to let a stranger's ill-informed opinion invade her emotions, but it had, and there wasn't much she could do to shake off the resulting doubts.

Once she was inside, they only kept growing. She hadn't been aware of developing a preconceived image of her birth father until she walked into his home and had that image contradicted so strongly. Absurdly, she felt let down. Had she imagined she possessed some great insight and empathy into his character by virtue of shared genes alone? And exactly what had she expected? A homely, slightly ramshackle dwelling full of old-fashioned implements? Maybe a wood cooking-stove, and an old iron bed covered in quilts? Kerosene lamps? Well, this cabin was anything but ramshackle. Rustic, yes, but also modern, with an electric range, thank you very much.

Since her arms were full of groceries, Alex sought the kitchen area first. She liked the open shelving filled with plain crockery, the plank flooring, and the scrubbed pine table surrounded by four ladder-back chairs. The living area was sparsely furnished with a small high-backed sofa covered in dark velvet and a matching armchair with ottoman. Everything faced the stone fireplace wall, where a display case mounted over the mantelpiece held arrowheads and small flint tools.

Indian artefacts. A locking wood cabinet against one wall contained more of them—several tomahawks, a stone mortar and pestle, a small pair of beaded moccasins, and an array of knives, their blades shaped from flint and tied with rawhide strips to handles carved from bone or horn. Three blankets graced the walls in lieu of more traditional decoration. The largest, hung at an angle, was faded and frayed. The smaller ones—probably saddle blankets—were in better colour and condition.

Aside from the collections, Alex saw no personal items. She was disappointed to find the loft bedroom as spare as the lower level. There was a large brass bed covered with a down quilt, a plain mirrored dresser, and an oak wardrobe. An octagonal window faced the woods, uncovered but high enough in the wall to provide privacy. A banister kept the loft safe, while allowing heat up from the living-room below.

This was very cosy, simple yet appealing. Alex sat down on the bed and ran a hand over the quilt, trying for a moment to imagine her mother living here with Tyson Conway, but of course she couldn't. To place Elise Stevens, serenely made up and dressed to the nines, in this rustic setting would be like putting an orchid in a cigar box.

Maybe that's why she left, Alex thought.

She went downstairs again, still puzzling. She'd have to get used to that. If she had been back in her apartment she would be watching the evening news, but here there was no television. She'd get used to that too. Probably even enjoy it. She could imagine no better atmosphere for serious thinking...or soul-searching, either, if it came to that. But for the time being she had no greater ambitions than to make a nice salad and enjoy the quiet.

She ate slowly, sitting in a twig rocker on the front porch, watching the sun trail down the sky, feeling the feeble heat of it struggle with the chill of early-spring air. As long as she stayed directly inside the sun's rays she was reasonably warm and even a tiny bit drowsy, and so she sat there and gazed indolently around her at the greenly wooded hill-top and thought that this might be a nice place to spend the next four weeks after all, and that if she moved inside very carefully and got to bed with the minimum of fuss she might just make it to sleep without a pill tonight.

But, once she'd brushed her teeth and washed in the little bathroom tucked under the stairs, shadows were falling. The living-room seemed almost macabre with Indian lore, and the bedroom was chilly and strange. She stripped to her underwear and slid under the down quilt, but it was no use. Although her body was drooping from the day's tensions, her eyes weren't. Resolutely, she fished about the floor for her handbag, found the prescription bottle and shook a pill into her hand. It was tiny and she swallowed it without water, then lay back down to wait.

You're a wreck, Alex, she told herself disgustedly. A real wreck.

CHAPTER TWO

ALEX was no stranger to dreams. Every night they ran the gamut from mildly perplexing to outright terrifying, although she rarely remembered anything in the morning beyond the emotions. The thing was...this time her dream was a stranger to her. If not she would have remembered him in vivid detail. He was gorgeous, she thought achingly, the kind of man that you never met in real life, or if you did he belonged to someone else, or was aeons out of your league, like a film star or a foreign power.

There was moonlight in her dream and she studied the man silently, trying to pin down just what feature made him so gorgeous. His eyes? They were brown, she thought, although it was difficult to tell. Yes, definitely brown, as were his hair and his beard, slightly wavy and both neatly trimmed. His face was strong and slim, and it seemed to be tanned wherever it wasn't covered with hair. He wore a plaid flannel shirt; beneath it his shoulders were broad, and he seemed to be tall, although again it was difficult to be sure with him sitting on the edge of her bed. She didn't care if he was six-feet-six, and she flashed him a little smile to tell him so.

'Welcome back,' he said in a husky, deep voice, but didn't return the smile.

'Back from where?' Alex murmured. She couldn't think straight...could you ever really think in a dream? His touch seemed so real that she could actually feel his fingertips pressed into her shoulder. Had he been shaking her?

'You tell me.' He frowned at her first question. 'I had a hard time waking you.'

'I'm not awake,' Alex told him, certain that she wasn't.

'How many did you take?' He gestured towards the pill bottle toppled on the nightstand. She hadn't put the cap on properly, and little white tablets had spilled everywhere.

'Only one.'

'Are you sure?'

He was still frowning. Alex stared at him for a long moment before breaking into a small smile that both mocked and blessed her imagination. Well, well, well. She'd dreamt someone to protect her. She hadn't been aware, until now, of how much she missed that. How long had it been since anyone had asked, 'Alex, are you eating right?' or felt her forehead, or even told her that she looked terrible? She knew she'd lost weight and there were shadows under her eyes, and that she was an insomniac without those little pills, but it was ridiculously gratifying to have someone else worry about her... even an imaginary man. 'I only ever take one,' she assured him.

'Why?'

'Why?' Alex blinked in surprise. 'Because I can't sleep.'

'Why can't you sleep?' He was taking her pulse now. Alex closed her eyes against the pleasure of his touch and he immediately tugged on her arm. 'No, you don't. Wake up.'

She stared at him. 'Are you a doctor?'

'No, a teacher.' He leaned closer to look into her eyes, and she melted a bit. He smelled wonderful... a little like aftershave, but mostly just male, clean and warm. 'How did you get in here?'

Shouldn't she be asking him? 'Jake gave me the key.'

'That figures,' he muttered. 'When are you expecting him?'

'Jake?' Alex raised an eyebrow. 'I'm not.'

He was frowning again. If he looked that sexy frowning, she couldn't wait to see a smile. 'Then suppose you tell me why he sent you up here? He knew I was coming home tonight.'

Alex blinked, trying to understand how one person could be responsible for another's dream. But working out the logistics proved too much for her, and Jake wouldn't be that nice to her anyway, would he? Sighing, she passed both palms across her face and pushed her hair back from her temples. 'Do you have to ask so many questions?'

'Just tell me why you're here.'

'I did tell you. Didn't I?' She suddenly felt vague about it, trailing off, then flushing because he looked so impatient. 'I'm not waiting for *him*.'

There was a stunned pause, then he muttered, 'Good grief!' He seemed amused in a black way. 'What has that brother of mine cooked up now?' He lifted a pale strand of hair that she'd missed and tucked it back off her cheek. 'Don't take this personally, honey, but whatever it is I'm just not interested. Not tonight, anyway. I've been driving for hours and I'm dead tired, and, as pretty as you look, lying there, I'm afraid I'm going to have to pass.'

Her own dream and she was being rejected? She looked pretty, but he'd pass? It was too humiliating. 'What kind of man are you?' she asked flatly, but with a wealth of meaning.

'One who prefers to choose his own women.'

'You wouldn't choose me?'

Her chin jutted out, small and slightly pointed... like a pixie's, Grandfather had once said. The man caught it neatly in his cupped palm. 'I wouldn't *pay* for you,' he told her.

'Oh. *Oh*. Was she a *prostitute* in this dream? If she was then she certainly was not earning her money, because she could barely move a muscle. Even if she could, she wouldn't sleep with a man that arrogant, not even in her dreams... would she? He was still holding her face, but his thumb had strayed to her bottom lip, stroking across it. 'I assume Jake *is* paying you, one way or another?' She must have stiffened, because he added thoughtfully, 'Or are you just in this for a good time?'

A good-time girl? she thought whimsically. It was only a slight improvement, but his hand felt so good on her face that she managed to forgo any offence. She closed her eyes briefly, trying not to show her pleasure, and when she opened them again he seemed to have leaned a little closer over her. 'I thought you were going to pass,' she reminded him.

'I am,' he said, but didn't move. 'I don't know you.' As if he couldn't help himself, he brought his other hand up so that her face was cradled between his palms. 'But what am I going to do with you? If you weren't halfway out of it I'd send you back to my brother. Or else have him come fetch you. I ought to do it anyway.' She saw another flash of dark amusement, then his voice roughened. 'I don't know why it should matter to me whether he takes advantage of you.'

Alex shivered. '*Does* it matter?'

'Oh, yeah,' he drawled, the mockery aimed inwardly. 'That's the curse of a gentleman—everything matters.' With an odd grimace he sat up and began undoing the buttons of his shirt. 'There's one thing you'd better understand, though. I'm not one hundred per cent gentleman, and never have been. So it's up to you to behave yourself.'

'What are you doing?' Alex breathed. The shirt was being stripped off strong shoulders. The white vest followed, and as his hands moved to the buckle of his belt her blue-grey eyes grew round. 'You're undressing!' she got out incredulously.

The man paused, but only to remove heavy walking boots and socks instead. Then the cord trousers came off. Mercifully, he was wearing briefs, because as soon as he'd skinned the cords off long muscled legs he lifted the covers and slid under them. 'Move over, honey.'

Alex vaulted to the outermost edge of the mattress. She also sat up, clutching the quilt under her chin. 'You can't sleep here.' The sight of his near-naked body unnerved her, but that was nothing compared to the trauma of having it in the same bed, under the same covers. 'You have to get out of here,' she told him frantically. Dream or no dream, she was not equipped for this.

'Look,' he raised himself on an elbow, 'isn't it a little ridiculous, you ordering me out of my own bed?' *His* bed? But, before she could deny that, he went on in a reasonable tone, 'You came here planning to sleep with me, didn't you? Well, that's what you're going to do...*sleep* with me. Unless you want to move downstairs.'

'If you were anywhere *near* one hundred per cent *you'd* move downstairs.'

He laughed shortly. 'Sweetheart, cast your fuzzy little mind back to my living-room. You should realise that you can't fit a six-foot-two man on a five-foot sofa. On the other hand, you'd probably fit.'

'Down there with the spirits?' Alex shuddered. 'No, thanks.'

'Then shut up and go to sleep,' he suggested blandly.

'I can't.' Alex pleated the sheet through her fingers. 'I've never slept with a man before.'

The brown eyes that had wearily closed only seconds before shot open. 'Holy Mirandum!' he groaned, pulling his body to a half-sitting position again. 'I'm going to wring Jake's neck!' He looked her over sharply. 'I should have guessed...the sleeping pills,' he tacked on in disgust. Then his eyes narrowed and his fingers locked round her upper arm. 'Exactly how old are you?'

Alex stared and, when he shook her a little, blurted honestly, 'Twenty-two.'

'Is that the truth?' He stared back, finally dropping introspectively against the pillows. 'I'm going to wring his neck anyway. But first I'm going to get some sleep, and you're going to stay on your side of the bed and keep quiet,' he warned.

But Alex was already edging off the mattress, carefully tucking the quilt around her. 'I'm going downstairs.'

'No, you're not.' The hand gripped her arm again, pulling her back. 'You're going to lie right here and see what it's like sharing a bed with a man you don't know. I doubt you'll have a better opportunity to learn whether you're cut out for this kind of work——' she could hear the grimace in his voice '—without actually getting *into* this kind of work. Besides that, I don't own a spare blanket and I'm not giving you mine.' As she subsided he muttered insultingly, 'You'd probably kill yourself on the stairs anyway, dumb kid.'

Alex lay stiffly, staring at the wood ceiling with its exposed beams. Tears stung her eyes, but until she heard his breathing deepen she made no move to wipe them away. She didn't want to wake him. *If* he was asleep. *If* he was even there. This is it, girl, she told herself sharply. You're finally losing your mind. Hallucinating. She turned on to her side, with her back to the man, and her eyes fell on to the bottle of sleeping tablets. Had she taken a pill tonight? If she had she would be sleeping now instead of going crazy, wouldn't she? She couldn't think... couldn't remember... but the prescription had been freshly filled before she left Louisville. If she counted them and one wasn't missing...

She reached out a hand a bit desperately as the idea occurred. Almost immediately the man's fingers were clamped over hers. He actually pried the bottle from her fist. Leaning over her to gather up the spilled tablets, he swiftly recapped the container, then threw it with suppressed force over the banister rail. A matter of seconds, then he was staring, very severely, into her eyes. 'Do you want to sleep forever?' he gritted, and shook her to emphasise the point.

'Why did you...?' Alex could hear the plastic bottle bouncing across the pine floor below. Nervously she wet her mouth. 'I didn't remember whether I took one.'

'Oh, you did,' he snorted. 'Believe me, you did.' He was right over the top of her. She could feel his breath on her cheek, and he had to be real, didn't he? She never dreamed like that... with all her senses alive. Her heart was beating so *fast*. *Too* fast. Like a child, she screwed her eyes shut and thought, Make him go away.

When she opened them he was still there. Tears gathered on her lashes and spilled. Weak tears. She was a weak person, after all. Hadn't Robert said so? Now here she was, about to be raped or killed, and she couldn't fight because she had drugged herself. All she could do was stare at the man in her bed, and think that Robert had been right about that, too. She *was* a terrible judge of character. She must be, because from the moment she'd opened her eyes to this man she had trusted him.

Already her pulse was slowing. She stared up into that handsome, frowning, but intrinsically gentle face, and said quietly, as if she was placing her life in his hands, 'Please don't hurt me.'

He held himself still, frowning down at her for what seemed like a long moment. 'Who are you?' he asked intently.

Alex bit her lip and looked away from him. It was a perfectly legitimate question. There was no reason for her to feel this way... as if her insides were tightening and tearing... as if her throat were clamped shut. She thought of Robert, shouting. She thought of her mother, so beautiful, so often withdrawn. She thought of Grandfather Bannon with his white moustache. Then she thought of Ty Conway and whispered wrenchingly, 'I just don't know any more.'

'Ah, *hell*,' the man groaned and rolled back on to his side. Snaking a slow arm around her middle, he pulled her, unprotesting, into the curve of his body. 'Go to sleep, honey. We'll talk in the morning.'

I can't, Alex thought. He moved his palm gently up and down on her stomach, the way one might comfort a little child. She could feel his heart beating into her back, and his breath stirring across her hair, and she realised that she no longer felt threatened. I *am* crazy, she thought, and rested against him. She felt safe.

Alex rolled over and cautiously stretched a hand out to the side. She felt a little silly after she'd done that... groped around for a body. There wasn't one, of course. Weak morning sunshine fell across her face, and she covered her eyes with both hands, savouring that last moment of drowsiness, remembering how prolifically she'd dreamed, and how peacefully she'd slept afterwards when she'd thought she was cradled in a strong pair of arms.

Stretching and smiling, she thought wickedly, Now I know how Scarlett felt the morning after. Well, not quite, but I can imagine how she felt. And it makes me wonder why I have to freeze off every man who speaks to me.

But the morning was too perfect for analysing. She'd slept—glory be!—and the day felt delicious... crisp, not cold, with blue sky floating beyond the octagonal window. She sat up against the pillows with the quilt wrapped round her shoulders, bracing herself to dive out for her clothes. *I could get used to this place, Ty Conway. It has a lot going for it. Solitude, trees all around, little birds singing to wake me up, endless quiet hours stretching ahead with no deadlines to make my stomach churn. In fact*... she realised with surprise... she was even hungry. Ravenous, really. There was something about the tang of wood smoke and the smell of coffee guaranteed to wake up an ar——

Alex felt the blood draining out of her face. Coffee? She sniffed the air and then stealthily drew back the covers and reached for her clothes. That was definitely coffee she smelled, and it was far too aromatic to have carried from a neighbour's house, even if there were a neighbour close enough, which there wasn't. Frantically she pulled the skirt over her head, then the sweater, before standing up to deal with the waistband zip. She shrugged into her jacket, but left her shoes alone. Better to be short and quiet.

On stockinged feet she padded slowly to the stairs. From the banister rail she caught a glimpse of a dark head and a strong back covered in plaid flannel, and her insides began to quake. She clutched the handrail tightly, but only made it halfway down before the man heard her and turned. A tall man, handsomely bearded, strange and yet familiar. '*You,*' she breathed, her colour leaving again.

Brown eyes passed the length of her, then rested intently on her shocked face. 'Good morning, Alexandra.'

Well. What should she do now? It seemed a little ridiculous to run. Instinct told her that he wouldn't hurt her. He'd had all night to hurt her, if that were his intention. Oh, lord, he'd had all *night*. Her legs went weak just thinking about it. And what was he doing here, in her father's cabin, anyway? She meant to ask him, but to her horror blurted out instead, 'So I didn't dream you.' Biting her lip, she tacked on accusingly, 'And how do you know my name?'

She thought she saw a corner of his mouth twitch as if he wanted to smile, but he didn't. Wise man. Shrugging, he delved a hand into his pocket and brought out her prescription bottle. 'It's printed on the label. Too bad I didn't think to look last night. It would have cleared up the misunderstanding.'

'Not for me,' Alex got out. 'I *knew* I wasn't a prostitute.'

This time she definitely saw a twitch. 'I owe you an apology for that.' he sobered. 'I didn't realise you were Ty's daughter.'

Alex stared at him. 'It seems to me that, if you realise who I am, then you must also realise that you owe me another apology...for trespassing. I still don't know who you are, or why you're here.'

'Jay McGee,' he said simply. 'I live here.' Her mouth opened in protest, but before she could voice it, he went on, 'Give me a chance, honey.' She shut her mouth and saw another glint of humour in his eyes. 'There's an easy explanation,' he told her: 'you're in the wrong cabin.'

'What?' Her mouth was dropping open again. 'Well, that's impossible,' she said stubbornly. She knew she'd followed Jake's directions exactly. This had to be the right place. 'The key fits.'

'The key that Jake gave you,' he said with the quiet air of a man who knew he was right. '*My* key.'

'Why would he have given me your key?'

'Because he keeps an eye on the place while I'm away and in return he's free to stay here when he feels like it...usually when he's entertaining a lady,' he pointed out, explaining his first assumption of last night: that she'd been waiting for his brother.

'Oh,' Alex said, her mind working crazily. '*Oh*,' her eyes widened, 'he *deliberately* sent me to your cabin. That's what John Shawn was trying to tell me.' She remembered the boy's hesitation, the way his uncle had cut him off when he'd tried to intervene.

'He's a pretty straight kid,' Jay McGee reinforced her opinion. 'Jake is a different story. Just what did you do to him?' At her blank look, he persisted, 'I know my brother. You must have done something. Otherwise no power on earth would have him sending a girl like you my way. Not even on my birthday.'

'It's your birthday?' Alex murmured distractedly.

'Yeah. What did you do to him?'

'I didn't *emasculate* him,' Alex groaned, wondering why she should feel so defensive. 'But any man using a line like that deserves to have his ego dented.'

He watched her for a few seconds, then slowly leaned back against the kitchen counter, arms crossed over his chest. 'What kind of line do you prefer, Alexandra?' His voice was perfectly even, but body language told her that she had offended him. Insulted his darned brother, probably.

'I don't know.' She blinked. She *didn't* know... she'd never really thought about it. 'Maybe I'd prefer no line at all,' she offered consideringly. '"I've been waiting for you all my life" sure doesn't work.'

To her relief, she saw a hint of a smile break through. 'Believe it or not, my brother Jake is *very* popular with the ladies.'

I'll bet so are you, Alex thought. An unwanted flashback assaulted her; she remembered exactly how it had felt snuggling into his chest, holding on to the hand that had rested in the centre of her body, murmuring 'I just don't know any more' like a lost teenager. Wrestling with that pill bottle. He had seen her at her absolute worst, pathetic and dependent and vulnerable.

Suddenly her legs began shaking, her face flamed, and she sat down on the third stair. 'Your brother Jake also knows how to exact revenge,' she muttered self-deprecatingly. For a moment she dropped her face into her hands, and she heard Jay McGee laugh softly.

'And how! But don't be embarrassed. It wasn't your fault.'

Fine for him to say. He hadn't spent the night with a strange man, dressed only in a lace bra and scanty briefs, rendered helpless and silly by a sleeping pill. But he had been at a disadvantage, too, hadn't he? Feeling a little better, she raked her hair back off her face and asked him softly, 'May I go with you?'

'Where?' He raised a brow.

'To wring Jake's neck. You said you were going to.'

Jay shook his head. 'You might do too good a job.'

'Then I think I'll go wash my face instead,' she said drily, and made her escape into the bathroom. She came out a few minutes later, combed and washed and prepared to take her leave gracefully, but he was there, handing her a mug of coffee, persuading her to stay for breakfast.

'You have to,' he coaxed. 'I've used all your groceries.'

He moved back to the range to stir his scrambled eggs. Alex saw that he had bread under the grill for toast. It smelled delicious, the coffee tasted delicious, and, as she curled her fingers more closely around the mug after taking that first sip, she realised that she was still ravenous, and that she wanted to stay.

'I'll show you the way to Ty's afterwards. It's just up the road.'

Still dazzled a bit by that grin, she pulled out a kitchen chair and sat down. Morning sun was streaming in from all directions, slanting across the pine floor and the tiled counter-tops and the unadorned stairs. The cabin smelled lemony and looked surprisingly clean...spotless, really...for a place that had been in a man's care.

'You have a very nice home,' she commented idly.

'Thanks. I built it myself, with a lot of help from my brothers. It makes a great retreat weekends and summers. I've got a few acres of woods to roam and my family close by. Can't ask for much more than that.'

'Where do you teach?'

'I'm surprised you remember that.' He lifted a brow, then, as if reluctant to embarrass her again, went on, 'I teach Kentucky history at the University of Louisville. I live in an apartment just off campus most of the year.'

'When does the term end?' Alex asked. She was thinking, Right in my back yard. This man has been right on my doorstep all along, but I spend my mornings running, my days working, and my evenings trying to write. I never meet anyone unless I'm scheduled to interview him. I have to get out more.

'I have a week of spring break,' Jay was saying, 'then four more weeks of school.'

'What do you do summers?'

There was a pause while he took the toast out of the oven and began to butter it. 'I teach a night class at the high school. Otherwise I help out on my mother's farm. It takes the whole family to plant the crops and garden, then keep them watered and weeded and de-bugged.'

Alex wondered whether he was talking down to her...a city girl. 'Are we talking about large-scale farming?' she asked, sipping her coffee.

'Fairly small-scale these days.' He shrugged. 'My father made his living at it, but times have changed. My mother sold about half the land after he died, partly because farming isn't as profitable as it once was, but mainly because my brothers and I have our own lives and spare time doesn't stretch all that far. Now we plant enough garden to fill the pantry with vegetables, raise enough livestock to keep meat in the freezer, and grow enough corn and hay to feed the livestock. The tobacco is meant to be an income crop, but, with today's market, who knows?' He shrugged again; she was finding the gesture very attractive, and the conversation interesting. 'My youngest brother Josh still lives at home and works the farm full-time,' he told her while filling two plates with steaming eggs. 'The rest of us pitch in when we can.'

Alex thanked him when he set her breakfast in front of her, and asked, with her fork already poised for the first bite, 'How many McGees are there, anyway?'

'Too many to name,' he assured her with a crooked smile. 'I have five brothers living, four of them married with kids. There's also my mom, of course, and an assortment of aunts and uncles and cousins. The McGee who settled this town was a prosperous old fellow.'

'While the Conway line has died,' Alex contrasted thoughtfully. 'Kate told me that the county is named for one of my ancestors.'

'Zebediah Conway, in 1810,' Jay supplied, watching her for a moment. 'And the line hasn't died. There's still you.'

Alex had no answer for that. She picked up a piece of toast and delicately bit off a corner. Jay tasted his eggs. They both sat eating in silence until the pause stretched so far that it was difficult re-entering the conversation. 'You haven't mentioned him,' Jay finally said, quietly, and she could tell that he had been thinking it for the last few minutes. Her father. Ty Conway.

Alex stared at her plate, then looked him in the eye. 'I didn't know him. It's hard to talk about him.'

'Can I help?'

She hesitated, knowing it was a sincere offer. Maybe she should be burning with curiosity, but what she actually did feel was more low-key than that. Confused and saddened, but little else. She didn't know how to explain, and, because he seemed to expect burning curiosity, she asked, 'Did you know him well?' Her voice sounded dull.

'Well enough,' he said without elaborating. He studied her thoughtfully instead, one large hand cupped round his coffee-mug, his body sprawled casually in the kitchen chair, his back straight, but one leg crossed over the other, ankle to knee, so that the muscles in his thighs stretched the cord trousers taut. Alex liked his hands, brown and sinewy. His face was arresting, strong yet fine-boned, the eyes almost a golden brown. She wasn't quite sure what she read in them. 'Why are you here, Alexandra?' he asked her softly.

'He left me the property.'

'I know.' Of course. It was in the newspaper. 'But that doesn't tell me anything. You could have sold it, sight unseen.'

Yes, she could have, if she'd been born without a conscience. 'He wanted me to spend some time here.' She shrugged uncomfortably. And I needed to get away, she admitted drily to herself, though not aloud.

'Ty loved this time of year best. He was happiest in spring, with all the trees budding... the grass pushing up. He'd spend hours pottering around the yard.' A shadow crossed Jay's face. 'Remembering, I guess.'

'Then he had an advantage over me,' Alex said, shocking herself with her own bitterness. 'I didn't even *know*. I didn't know there was a Ty Conway until Kate told me. It seems a little ironic that he knew where I was and how to contact me, but didn't, and now that he's dead I'm supposed to feel some kind of sentiment for this property... for him.'

She didn't know why she'd betrayed herself that way. Jay McGee was a stranger, and, to lessen his chances of understanding, a friend of her birth father's. She was surprised when he didn't bristle. 'If I had a daughter who hadn't seen me for twenty years,' he told her quietly, 'I wouldn't want her only memory to be of a dying man, or a funeral.'

'But before that.' She waved a hand helplessly. 'Why not get in touch before?'

'I can't answer that.' He shook his head. 'Maybe he thought you were happier not knowing. Or maybe he thought it was your mother's privilege——'

'My mother died four months ago,' Alex cut in tonelessly.

'I'm sorry.'

'So am I.' She bit her lip, but gradually regained control. 'My father... my *adoptive* father,' she tautly corrected, 'died in the same accident. That left no one but Uncle Stuart to clue me in. He deeply resented the imposition, yet managed in about ten words to get his point across. It seems I was the Bannon family skeleton.'

'Alexandra...'

'Call me Alex.' She shifted restlessly in her chair.

'Alex,' he began again, his eyes probing, 'the way you talk, it's as if you're *ashamed* of the past.'

'Only because *they* were,' she came back heatedly. 'After my mother left him—my real father—she wasn't even welcome at my grandfather's house. Not with a broken marriage and a child, anyway,' she tacked on for emphasis. 'So we went to live with my Great-Aunt Elsa in Wilmington where a nanny kept me out of sight while Mother re-entered society and became engaged to Robert.' She paused to lick her dry lips. 'We were welcomed to Louisville after they married... legitimised, you might say. To protect their standing in the community my relatives fostered the belief that we were a family by natural means. Robert took a position in my grandfather's company.' She shrugged. 'He managed to pull it off.'

Jay's eyes flashed angrily. 'You mean hide the fact that his wife was briefly married to a poor mountain man and had a child with him?'

'Scandalous stuff,' Alex agreed flatly. She felt foolish. Cheated and deceived.

'Did you always call him Robert?' Jay asked.

'Not always.' She moved uncomfortably. 'I called him Dad until I was about twelve.'

'What happened?'

She didn't feel up to relating that particular story. She'd given him too much raw material already. 'I'll tell you some time,' she demurred. 'Right now, will you tell me something?'

'If I can.'

'What do the people here think?' She leaned intently towards him. 'I mean, what do they know about me?'

'To answer that, Alex, let me tell you something about Ty. First of all, he was a good man, the kind of man that anyone would be proud to call a friend. He'd do anything to help a friend, and there wasn't a better listener in this county if you wanted to talk to someone and have your thoughts kept safe. But Ty wasn't a talker. I know that his wife left him and eventually remarried. I know that he allowed her to make a new life for you in exchange for news from time to time. I know that he missed both of you,' he said huskily, 'and that's not something he told me, but something I saw for myself.'

Alex felt moisture prick her eyes, blinked and bent her head over her plate to hide her reaction. She carried a bite of scrambled egg to her mouth purely out of reflex. The food was cold and she pushed the rest of it slightly away. 'So there are a lot of gaps in the story,' she reflected. 'Am I going to be called upon to fill them?'

'That's up to you.' He shrugged and drained the last of his coffee. 'Naturally people will be curious. More importantly, they'll be willing to tell you about Ty. If you're interested.'

'I'm interested, ' she said. 'I just don't think I can meet expectations. I may be the long-lost daughter coming home, but I don't feel like it. I feel disconnected, as if this is happening to someone else.'

'Give yourself time,' he suggested gently.

'Your brother thinks I'm a mercenary.'

He grinned a little. 'Did he say that before or after you flattened his ego?'

'After.'

'Honey, what did you expect?'

With an image of Jake McGee in her mind, Alex blurted out, 'Is he an Indian?'

Jay laughed outright at that. 'We all are. Our great-grandmother was full-blooded Cherokee. That makes us one-eighth Indian and proud of it, although Jake is the only one among my brothers and me who got the physical characteristics. On the other hand, you should see my mother.' His brows rose expressively. 'Her hair is coal-black and falls below her waist when she takes the pins out, and her eyes are so dark that they're like mirrors.'

'So that explains your interest in Indian artefacts.'

Alex threw out the phrase as statement cum query, but Jay did not rise to the bait. 'That's part of it,' he agreed instead. 'And you may not be aware of this, Alex, but old Zebediah Conway took an Indian bride. Somewhere in your veins there's a drop of Cherokee blood just waiting to be acknowledged.'

'You're joking!' She stared at him, halfway sure that he was. Her extremely fair colouring came compliments of a set of great-grandparents who had immigrated from

Norway; nothing about her suggested an Indian ancestry. 'You *are* joking?' she said again, uncertain.

'No, it's a fact.' Jay watched her for a moment, then held out a hand, palm up. 'So how about it, Alexandra? Want to have a look?'

CHAPTER THREE

JAY knew his subject well. Alex listened with heightened interest as he identified the flint tools and explained how each was used. Everything had a specialised purpose...cutting, grating, grinding, sewing. She particularly admired the long, thin bone needles and the small flat scrapers with their hollows for thumb and forefinger. The collection was extensive and, unless Alex missed her guess, quite valuable.

Examining a primitive bone-handled knife, she asked neutrally, 'Where do you find things like this?'

Jay shrugged and went down on his haunches to stoke the fire. 'Here and there.'

Alex was not surprised by the reticence in his tone. The retrieval and sale of Indian grave goods had come under heated scrutiny a few years before and remained a bitter issue. Protestors despised the practice and labelled it desecration, while dealers fought to keep their decades-long businesses and often their livelihoods from falling under siege. Collectors, too, faced heavy criticism. A man who bought or sold grave goods was considered by some to be just as guilty as the man who unearthed them.

Alex believed any human resting place to be hallowed. She'd discovered that self-truth—perhaps unfortunately—while on her first assignment for Robert, where she'd found the mining of a mass grave site so personally abhorrent that she'd lost all sight of objectivity. Her notes and taped interviews had wound up on a staff writer's desk for completion; that was her orientation to Robert's ruthless editing style.

She fingered the long edge of the knife and imagined a warrior who roamed the spirit world unarmed. Not every relic, of course, came from a burial site. Some turned up at ancient camp grounds or caves which had once provided shelter.

She searched Jay's eyes when he straightened, choosing to give him the benefit of the doubt. 'Careful.' His voice was smooth and deep, his touch on her shoulder disturbing. 'The blade is still sharp.'

Alex made a small sound in her throat, half-groan, half-sigh, and at his quizzical look invented, 'I was just wondering what your great-grandmother would have thought about my food processor.'

His grin made her legs a little weak. 'She would have distrusted anything that easy.' He accepted the knife from Alex and replaced it. 'I'll go pack up your groceries...or what's left of them. Breakfast was on the stove before I realised that Jake would never be thoughtful enough to stock my refrigerator.'

Alex readily dismissed the apology. 'My providing the food was only fair trade for your cooking it. I enjoyed the meal.' She stood a bit awkwardly in the kitchen doorway, watching him put her things back in the brown paper bag. 'I'm sure I can find the cabin on my own, Jay. I don't want to put you out...no more than I have already, I mean.'

'It's no problem,' he insisted easily. 'I'd like to check the flue before you use the wood stove. I can ride over with you and walk back.'

Alex nodded. Actually, she'd prefer to be alone for her first look at the cabin, but it would have been rude to make any further excuses. Not to mention the fact that she knew nothing about flues or wood stoves, except that they were comforting on a chilly day.

She gathered up her vanity case and handbag, and preceded Jay out to her car, admiring his sleek black Blazer parked alongside it. She noticed that the back was full of boxes, clothes, and books. 'I could help you unload your things.'

'Thanks for offering,' Jay declined, 'but you'll be getting settled yourself.' He stowed the grocery bag in the rear seat, then Alex's case. She wondered how he was going to fit his long legs into her little car, and in fact it was a crush until he found the lever that let the passenger seat back several notches. As Alex reversed rather nervously out of his drive he instructed, 'Take the next right.' The next right turned out to be a gravel lane that led into the trees only a few dozen yards past Jay's cabin.

'This *is* close.' Alex flung him a wry grin. 'Doesn't zoning law require half a mile between houses up here?'

'It must have seemed that way driving up. Actually, Ty sold me the property where my cabin sits. It used to be part of his homestead.'

'I see.' Alex considered the landscape before her. A row of bare trees lined the gravelled road, and there were more of them in the yard. Rings of rock marked the homes of several flowerbeds, and a weathered trellis supported some twisted growth, probably a rose bush. In contrast to the promise of a pretty yard, the dwelling ahead seemed forlorn, a very small log house with little to distinguish it from the shed at the back other than its covered front porch and small square windows. She parked the car beside a battered van and sat clenching the steering-wheel. Her chest suddenly felt tight.

Jay balanced the case and groceries with ease in one arm, and came around to open her door. 'Looks as if Jake has been here.' He gestured with his head towards the cabin. There, draped over the doorknob on a piece of twine, hung the key. 'At least I won't have to jimmy a window.'

Alex nodded, thinking Jake must now be tickled pink over his prank. In delivering the proper key he would have had to drive past Jay's house, and that meant he'd seen both their vehicles parked outside it. He knew they'd spent the night together. She could only shudder to think what he might do with *that* information.

She stood aimlessly on the porch while Jay unlocked the door. He stepped back to let her inside, surreptitiously watching her reaction... and frowning, although Alex didn't notice. She couldn't have known that her face had gone white. She was too full of the moment... the rather ghostly moment when she walked into that room and found every inch of it somehow familiar.

The iron bed was yellowed with time, its patchwork quilt faded. The small cooking stove was covered in aged soot, and the kerosene lamps on a thick shelf were topped with badly smoked chimneys. No surface dirt was in sight, thanks to Kate, yet the room emitted an air of neglect. A heavy cast-iron sink with hand-operated pump took up one end of the room, an old armoire the other. Alex passed slowly through the small doorway beside it to discover a bathroom that, judging by its low roof line, had been added after the original house was built. It consisted of an enormous old claw-footed tub, a small wall basin skirted in a faded cotton print, and a commode that flushed by virtue of a pull chain attached to an overhead water box. Alex stared at the clumsy, utilitarian fixtures and thought of her mother's *en suite* bathroom at home with its whirlpool tub, Italian ceramic tiles, and gold-plated faucets.

When she came back out into the main room her face was still pale. She sat down on the bed and stared at her clasped hands, trying to still that sick, fluttering sensation in her stomach, only looking up when she became aware of Jay's eyes on her. He'd unloaded the groceries into an ancient round-cornered refrigerator and now he was leaning against the sink, his face revealing very little, although his voice held a decided edge. 'Not what you expected, Alexandra?'

'No,' she breathed, too shaken to be offended by what he was apparently thinking... that she was disappointed with her humble inheritance. 'It's just the opposite, really.' Eyes troubled, she stressed slowly, 'This is *exactly* what I expected. It's... I... What I'm trying to tell you is that I feel as if I *remember* it.'

He frowned and shifted position slightly. She could understand his finding the idea objectionable. She thought it was crazy herself. 'I don't think you could, Alex. You were just a baby when your mother left Ty.'

'Ten months old,' she supplied, mouth twisting. 'I know.'

'There must be an explanation,' he said. 'How about Kate? Didn't she describe the place to you?'

'Not in any great detail. Not like this...' The sceptical look in his eyes still suggested that she might have let her imagination get the better of her. Frustrated, she tacked on with a singular lack of conviction, 'It's possible that I absorbed more from Kate than I realised.' She didn't believe that for one moment. The feeling of familiarity had hit her right in the gut. It was very real.

Jay didn't say any more on the subject. He began instead to pull the sections of stove-pipe apart and examine them. After he'd worked for a few moments he asked conversationally, 'What are your plans for today?' He'd spread a newspaper on the floor, but powdery soot still clouded the air over his head. With a wry grin that was meant to put them back on easy footing he added, 'Aside from cleaning, of course.'

Alex glanced about her in mild despair. 'I'd say the mess you're making is the least of my worries. Everything in here seems to be covered in a yellow film.'

'It's called a patina of age,' he corrected drily. 'Ty always cared more for the outside than the inside. Think you'll be around long enough to let it bother you?'

'I have a four-week leave from my job.'

His eyes crinkled lazily and almost speculatively at the corners, sending little shafts of warmth through her midsection. He didn't, however, pursue that avenue. Instead he asked, 'What do you do, Alex?'

'Didn't I tell you?' A few years ago family pride would have made certain that she'd told him, but she was no longer bursting with enthusiasm over her inherited field... a fact, in itself, that bothered her immensely. 'My family founded a regional magazine, *Kentucky!* Maybe you know it?'

He glanced up from a slightly rusted joint of pipe, something unreadable flickering in his eyes, disappearing. He studied her quietly for a moment before admitting, 'I used to be a subscriber.'

'Used to be?' Alex invited elaboration. 'What happened?'

'I dropped my subscription.' His shrug, although wry, was not an apology. 'When the format changed a couple of years ago I lost interest. Most of my favourite features were cut out or else altered so much that I no longer enjoyed the magazine.'

'Robert's initial approach to running things——' Alex got up from the bed and took a few steps towards the tiny kitchen area '—could be summarised in three phrases: shake them up, sift them out, and bring in new blood... lots of it. He was a completely different publisher from my grandfather, a fact that didn't go unnoticed by the subscribers. Readership took a fairly sharp decline during the first year, but we eventually picked the numbers back up from the political sector. Even topped them. An analytical man was Robert.'

'Each to his own,' Jay shrugged philosophically and tapped hard on the pipe, 'although if you ask me the man threw away the one unique quality that made *Kentucky!* a good regional journal. Human interest.' A huge clot of soot fell on to the newspaper and he squinted into the pipe again. 'I think that's got it.' Then, catching her off guard, 'You still haven't told me what you do, Alex.'

'I don't have a job description.' Her voice, for all its airy self-mockery, could not disguise a distinct brittle note. 'I hold this ambiguous position on staff. Not as an assistant precisely, not as an administrator...' she tipped her head and her hair fell like an opalescent pale curtain to one side '... not exactly as a public representative, although I've done my share of that on occasion. I once jokingly referred to myself as the token daughter,' she summed up flatly. 'Now I realise it was no joke.'

Jay began fitting the stove-pipe back into place without comment. Alex watched him, instantly regretting the bitterness that had spilled from inside her. She hadn't told him the truth, either, although the things she had told him were no lies. Robert had despised her writing. And Stuart's tolerance was bound to wane.

'Jay?' She suddenly forced a note of charm into her persona to counteract the brittleness of moments before.

'Yes, Alex?' He settled the base of the pipe into position and straightened, his smile faintly mocking, but very attractive. Alex was all too aware of his appeal without her heart doing that crazy little flutter of warning. And she didn't know why it had to be a *warning*. Maybe because her overworked nerves rejected the thought of any more strain.

'Would it be too great an imposition,' she rushed on, 'for you to show me how to build a fire in that thing?'

* * *

By the time Jay was satisfied with her efforts Alex looked almost as sooty as him, but the fire was crackling and the main room was starting to feel cosy. Preparing food would be another matter, Alex thought resignedly as she carried in a load of wood and kindling from the porch. The stove might be antiquated, but it was the only source of heat, cooking or otherwise, in the house, and Jay had warned her that, although it started slower than a modern range, it burned hotter in the end.

'There you go, honey.' He dropped his own arm-load of wood on to the stove mat and dusted his hands, unaware of how his casual endearments affected her. 'Is there anything else you need before I go?'

'Yes.' Alex made a rueful grimace over her new suit, brushing away the bits of bark that clung to it. 'The name of a good dry-cleaner.'

'Clean and Dry, on Main Street,' he prompted with a grin. 'You can't miss it—it's located at the only intersection with a traffic-light.'

'Thanks, Jay.' At the door she gave him a warm smile, wishing she had the courage to add 'for everything'. But she wasn't sure how he might react. Was it even proper etiquette to thank a man for behaving himself in an awkward situation? She compromised with, 'I think you're one hundred and ten per cent.' Then, because it was such a corny thing to say, she blushed.

Jay chuckled softly and without thinking captured her face between his hands. Then he laughed again because he'd put black fingerprints all over her. 'Oops. Sorry.' He tried to wipe away a smudge with the heel of his hand, but only succeeded in making it worse. 'No, it's not working. I don't think anything short of the bathtub is going to do.' His eyes were golden brown, positively alight with gentle humour, and in the midst of it, much to her pleasant shock, he dipped his head and brushed a warm kiss across her upturned mouth. 'It's been an honour meeting you. And Alex?' he asked huskily near her ear. 'You're very welcome.'

Staring after him when he left was for Alex an involuntary action, like breathing... or touching fingertips to her mouth where he'd kissed her. Intently silent, she noted the male beauty of his movements. He walked straight and tall, his legs eating up the hillside, muscles in his shoulders and back lightly flexing beneath faded cords as his arms swung in graceful rhythm. His hair took on coppery highlights from the morning sun, making her think of the way his beard had brushed her chin. She breathed a faint sigh as he disappeared from sight. She'd never expected to find a man like that up here.

Moving almost dazedly inside, she glanced around the dim little room and realised that Jay McGee still filled it. She'd barely given Ty Conway a thought.

She wasn't sure afterwards what prompted her cleaning frenzy. A desire to get her house in order? It *was* her house now... at least for the moment, and out of some form of loyalty to her birth father she tried to centre her mind on his home. She sat on the bed in lieu of a straight armchair in the corner that didn't look too comfortable, and skittishly re-examined her initial reaction. She found to her relief that the eeriness had passed. She was more inclined now to believe, as Jay had suggested, that Kate had described Ty's house to her, or else it was just one of those inexplicable coincidences. She lay back for several minutes against the faded old quilt and greying sheets that passed as bed linen, absently testing their rough texture between her fingertips, staring up at the exposed-beam ceiling that had aged to a blackened hue. Without even thinking she got up to strip the bed down to its ticking mattress and then walked back and forth, adding kitchen- and bath-towels to the pile, and removing the thin cotton curtains from the windows.

This place, she decided, was the victim of a man's haphazard housekeeping, and badly needed some deep-down attention. If she was going to stay here for the next month then she'd better start by buying detergent and bleach, and locating a laundry. She'd bring home some really strong pine cleaner, too, and tackle that patina.

The odd thing was that by the time she'd washed up and changed into jeans for the trip to town she was almost...just almost...viewing her brush with Conway County as a challenge. Perusing the supermarket shelves for cleaning supplies, she finally allowed herself the rest of the admission...that she had Jay to thank for her improved attitude. Standing in this same shop yesterday, she had been filled with a daunting sense of obligation—and belligerence, thanks to brother Jake—but little else.

The plump sales assistant was on duty again today, her hands buried deep in her pockets in an obvious gesture of reserve, her expression wary. 'Good morning,' she said formally. 'Will that be cash or charge?'

Alex unloaded her purchases on to the counter and coaxed her own voice, unfamiliar with polite diffidence, to respond, 'Cash, thanks. I was wondering...can you tell me where to find a laundry?' She looked up and tried on a friendly smile, feeling like the tin man who needed oil because the gesture took so much effort...and marvelling belatedly because it had been so easy with Jay. 'I need to wash an old quilt, so I'll need a super-capacity tub.'

The brunette sent back a cautious smile. 'Is it a really old quilt, hon?'

'From the looks of it.' Alex nodded.

'Then you don't want to put it in a *machine*. It might fall apart. What you need is some really mild soap. Soak your quilt in the bathtub overnight, then hang it out to dry. That will get it nice and fresh.' Alex followed the ample figure in its blue smock back down the detergent aisle. 'Here you go, hon. Directions are on the back.'

'Thank you,' Alex said gratefully, feeling as if a tiny corner of her soul had unfolded. How did I get to be so brittle in the first place? she despaired afterwards as she watched her laundry tumbling round and round the coin-operated drier. This isn't how I want to be...crackly around the edges and raw inside. This isn't normal.

However, her mind, for all its infinite circling around the point, did not interfere with her work. By the end of the afternoon she had scrubbed every inch of the walls, floors, and windows until the little house smelled like a pine forest. She bleached the bathroom from top to bottom, and soaked exhaustedly for a while in the tub afterwards. Then she put her quilt in to soak, making up the bed with just sheets for the time being...sheets which had come respectably white with a little care. Dressed only in a terrycloth robe, she was contemplating the contents of her suitcase when she heard a vehicle in the drive.

Jay. She was appalled by her quick pleasure upon catching sight of the Blazer through an unadorned window. Then just as quickly she became appalled by her appearance. She was scrubbed pink from the tub...covered only by a three-quarter-length white robe, albeit a decent one, barefoot and wet-haired. If she had been at home she would be monitoring his arrival through a doorman and an intercom; there would be plenty of time to dash and change before he made the journey in the lift. But here, having him in the driveway was only seconds away from having him on the front porch. There was nowhere to dash to, particularly once she realised that he had seen inside as easily as she saw out.

'Hi.' Jay gave her a crooked grin as she opened the door and stepped back to allow him entry. He looked her up and down, seeing not what she thought—a bedraggled female—but rather a slender young woman, swathed, barefoot, in pure white, with a tantalising glow to her skin and the tension of discomfiture behind her eyes. 'I've caught you at a bad time.'

'I've just got out of the tub,' Alex said unnecessarily. She ran a hand over her damp hair, undecided whether to be honest and embarrassed, or to attempt nonchalance. 'I can never clean house without getting most of the dirt on me.' She didn't add that she was something of a novice at housework. When growing up she'd had a maid at home to do the cleaning; it was only upon moving into her apartment that she'd branched out into domesticity.

Jay took a look around the living area, his face revealing approval and even slight surprise at the changes she'd made. 'You've been busy.'

She shifted from one bare foot to the other, pressing her toes into the freshly scrubbed oak boards. 'I haven't put the curtains back up yet.' Maybe she'd buy new ones, she thought half-heartedly. She was dying of embarrassment.

'Alex...' Jay hesitated, then smiled faintly '...I'm sorry if I've made you uncomfortable, but even in a bathrobe with wet hair and no make-up, believe me, you're the picture of class. Just pretend you're at the health club—how about that?'

Alex stared. She'd never met a man like this...one who insisted on ignoring all the accepted social standards for a kind of base-line frankness. The funny thing was, he'd gone a long way towards putting her at ease. She shut her mouth and then opened it again. 'Was there something you wanted, Jay?'

'Yes.' The smile twisted sideways, as if he was relieved that she'd taken his teasing in her stride, then hovered there, sexy as blazes. 'I'd like you to celebrate my birthday with me.'

Alex cast him a startled look before she could help herself, then bent over her wrist-watch in the hope that the swing of her hair might conceal the rest of her reaction... a mixture of disconcertedness and pleasure at his invitation. But she'd forgotten that wet hair didn't swing. She felt Jay's eyes on her face as she discovered with little interest that the time was a few minutes past five. 'What did you have in mind?' Looking up again, she managed to inject a casual note into her voice. 'Dinner?'

'Supper,' he corrected with crinkling eyes. 'A traditional McGee birthday supper at my mother's. This is your chance to meet everyone.'

'I see.' Alex thought of all those strange faces. She bit down on her lip in indecision. 'Will Jake be there?'

'I can't say that question surprises me.' Jay's soft laugh inexplicably made her blush. 'And no, my brother Jake won't be making an appearance. Saturday is his busiest night at the station. You're safe.'

A small smile flickered over her lips. 'I'm sure I'd be safe with you anyway.' *Flirting, Alex?* she asked herself disgustedly, but the scolding didn't have much impact. And it was virtually nullified when compared to Jay's answering smile, which felt like bubbles coursing through her veins.

Dragging her mind back to practical matters, she asked lightly, 'And what does one wear to a traditional McGee birthday supper?'

'Better make it something comfortable,' he suggested with wry humour. 'Something indestructible. Something that can take contact with a lot of kids.'

'How many kids?'

'Too many to count. I can't remember all their names.'

'Don't give me that,' Alex laughed, remembering that he'd used the same line that morning. 'Tell me about them.'

'I will,' Jay promised. Unaccountably his eyes began to darken. 'After you're dressed.'

The pause stretched out between them. Then Jay took a step towards her, and Alex was sure that he meant to kiss her again. She even started to lift her mouth before she realised that he had lightly grasped the lapels of her robe, not to draw her closer, but to tuck her gaping neckline back into place. His mouth quirked gently as quick colour touched her cheeks. 'I saw more last night, honey.'

Alex tightened her sash and stepped backwards, chin going up in defiance of the blush she could actually feel. 'I'm not your honey,' she told him, a marked lack of conviction in her voice.

'I know.' The smile still hovered behind his eyes as Jay added in a soft drawl, 'I'll have to see what I can do about that.'

CHAPTER FOUR

THEY had driven for perhaps eight minutes along a scenic route called River Bend when Jay put on his indicator and slowed the truck. 'Here we are,' he announced with quiet pride. 'Say hello to the McGee family farm.'

Alex surveyed the sweeping valley to their left. Amid a stand of weeping willows near the bottom sprawled a white two-storey house with black-shuttered windows and a long covered porch. Its red shingled roof was echoed by the painted tin that topped a massive barn and surrounding sheds. Whitewashed board fencing stretched in every direction, and through the distant tree-line Alex could make out a thin green ribbon of water. 'The Kentucky River?' Without waiting for an answer, she breathed, 'Do I see *horses* down there?'

'Yes, ma'am.' Jay's eyes were on her, enjoying her reaction. 'Watch this.' He rolled down his window and gave a long whistle, and Alex caught her breath as a magnificent colt let out a spirited whinny and thundered across the upper field. To her further elation, the animal raced Jay's truck the length of the gravel drive—a contest he easily won—then stood prancing and tossing his head until they caught up.

Jay parked the Blazer and held out a hand to Alex. 'Want to be introduced?' She slid across the seat after him, eyes glowing for the chestnut creature which had poked his curious head over the fence. She had to climb the bottom fence rail to see him properly, for, in spite of a certain babyish look to his features, the colt was quite large.

'Like him?' Jay's voice sounded husky, indulgent.

'I love him!' Alex slid her fingers under the wild black forelock, rubbing the whorl of short hair beneath. 'What's his name?'

'Brady. Thank my niece Meredith for that,' he added with dry humour. 'She's wild about animals... livestock, ducks, rabbits, racoons—you name it. Treats them like humans. She takes care of Brady when I'm not around.' He reached out to scratch the massive jaw. 'This guy is our pride and joy.'

'How old is he?'

'Not yet two.' Alex glanced sideways and found him right there, on eye level. She was so used to him towering over her that it was a kind of shock having his face so close. She froze momentarily on her stand, arrested by the fine, taut texture of his skin, the glint of his hair and beard in the evening sun. His eyes were warm brown, slightly narrowed, speculative. 'I didn't have you figured as a horse lover, Alex.'

'I don't know a thing about horses, but for some reason I adore them.' She avoided a rather vigorous nudge from Brady and added, 'As long as they stay on their side of the fence.'

'You never learned to ride?'

'The opportunity didn't come up.'

'I can fix that,' he offered.

'You mean *teach* me?'

His grin mocked the faint note of panic in her voice as he pointed out, 'I haven't lost a student yet.'

'I'll think about it.' She eyed the colt and noted uneasily that even half grown he'd make two or three of her. Her glance slid evasively around the side-yard. She realised that there were at least half a dozen vehicles parked with Jay's—two station wagons, a police car, and assorted pick-ups. Strains of animated conversation drifted through a raised window. The back door opened and shut.

A girl of perhaps fourteen or so was running towards them, face alight with smiles. 'You're here! Happy birthday!'

'It's about time the welcoming committee arrived.' Jay laughed and spread his arms wide for a hug. The girl was slight of build but a good two inches taller than Alex, with brown hair that tumbled thick and straight over her shoulders. When Jay set her on her feet again she planted a resounding kiss on his cheek. 'Meredith,' he grinned, 'say hello to a friend of mine. This is Alex Stevens. Alex, Meredith McGee.'

'Hi.' Jay's niece held out her hand and Alex shook it, liking the girl's blue-eyed good looks. 'My brother said he met you yesterday.'

Alex climbed down from the fence and brushed off the front of her trousers. 'You must mean John Shawn.' She glanced at Jay with a small smile. 'Yes, he gave me a fill-up at your uncle's service station. Nice boy.'

Meredith's eyes rolled expressively. 'You wouldn't say that if you knew him.' There was a noticeable pause before she asked, 'Are you really Ty's daughter?'

'Yes, I am.'

Alex had braced herself for questions, but no more came. 'I miss Ty,' the girl said softly instead. Her hand blindly found the colt's rough jaw. 'He always had an apple in his pocket for Brady.' She offered up a pensive smile. 'Would you like to ride him?'

'Some other time, thanks.' *Everyone has some special memory of him,* Alex was thinking. *Everyone except me.* 'I'm afraid I don't know how to ride. But Jay says he can teach me.'

'He taught Paula in only a couple of weeks.' A harmless enough remark, Alex thought, yet Meredith pulled a slight face at Jay as if to apologise for saying the wrong thing. A cryptic little message soon followed. 'You do know that she's coming to supper?' And then, as if to underscore the obvious when Jay failed to react, 'And Uncle Jake *isn't*?'

Jay smiled faintly. 'Do you think that might be a problem?'

Alex was completely intrigued by the way Meredith widened her eyes. 'Don't you?'

There were a lot of McGees. So many, in fact, that once inside the charming high-ceilinged living-room Alex needed all of her concentration to make sense of the introductions. She tried an old trick of Grandfather Bannon's... putting a key bit of information with each name in order to facilitate her memory.

Joshua, for instance, was the only full-time farmer. Brown-haired and brown-eyed like all the brothers, he had a quick, rather mischievous grin that warned Alex he might be a practical joker. His wife Caroline she labelled as shy and sweet, with russet-coloured hair and the palest green eyes she had ever seen.

Next came Joseph, a quiet man who had unwittingly made things easy by wearing his store logo. Beneath a matching Joe's Hardware shirt, wife Christina's tummy was out to *there*. 'Due in June,' she offered with a friendly grin. Her wind-blown light hair took the form of haloed curls with the tiny daughter who sat astride her hip. Jay paused to tickle the child's cheek, and Alex melted a little.

The tall man in sheriff's uniform was Kate's husband, Jonah, the ten-year-old before him their son Scott.

She had just enough time to learn that Kate was working before she found her hand being pumped in another grizzly-bear grip. She peered into John's pleasant, tanned face—creased in a few places and topped with very curly hair, cut short—and tried to imagine why Jay's eldest brother looked so familiar. Then her mouth flew open, and she asked weakly, 'You don't by any chance drive a monster log truck?'

'As a matter of fact, I do. I'll let you in on a little secret, Alex.' Eyes twinkling, the man leaned conspiratorially closer. 'Up here we share the road fifty-fifty.'

Alex heard a few splutters around the room. 'I barely had enough for myself, not to mention sharing! I hope you won't hold it against me.'

'Leave the poor girl alone.' That chiding female voice was connected to a round, bare face framed by short rippling curls. So this was where John Shawn and Meredith got their blue eyes. 'I'm Meg McGee,' the woman introduced herself. 'I do the book-keeping for John's logging business, when I'm not busy keeping him in line.'

'I'm pleased to meet you, Meg.'

'And that's everyone except the head of the family.' Jay led Alex to a slim figure standing quietly to the back of the group. Dropping an affectionate kiss to the woman's smooth cheek, he straightened to smile down on both of them, 'Mom, meet Alexandra Stevens. Alex, this is my mother, Laura McGee.'

The woman was simply dressed in a blue work shirt and navy jeans, her beautiful black eyes and sculptured cheekbones set off by a heavy twist of pure raven hair. 'It's good to see you again, Alexandra.' The Cherokee heritage was in strong evidence, yet oddly enough it was not Laura McGee's Indian blood that had the greatest effect on Alex, but rather the serene aura surrounding her. She held out her hand, and Alex found its grasp firm, yet gentle. 'Welcome back.'

The words took a moment to register. 'Back?' Alex echoed softly.

'Back to your birthplace. You were born in this house.' Jay's mother paused with a smile. 'I can see that surprises you. I'll tell you all about the circumstances later. When we have a chance to talk.'

'I'd like that very much,' Alex said. 'Thank you, Mrs McGee.'

'Call me Laura, please. Everyone does.'

Jay gave Alex's shoulder one last squeeze. She felt a moment's panic when his hand began slipping away. He couldn't consign her to all these strangers. They seemed like nice enough people, but what would she say to them? Worse, what would they say to her? Oblivious to her silent qualms, Jay drew up a chair and began talking with his brothers.

'Awful, isn't it?' Blonde Christina linked arms with Alex on their way to the kitchen. 'But ask yourself, do you really want to listen to all those hunting and fishing stories? Give me the girl-talk any day.'

'Don't you mean gossip?' Meg, tying an apron around her thick waist, laughed. 'Don't soft-pedal it, Chris.'

Her sister-in-law tossed back a sunny, philosophical grin. 'We all know gossip is the life-blood of this town. Why fight what you can't change?'

Alex, being a likely object for gossip herself, watched the children being shepherded off to play and halfway longed to join them. Suppose these women tried to pump her for personal details? How could she wriggle out of a friendly inquisition without offending Jay's family?

Casting an anxious eye about, she noted inconsequentially that Laura's neat one-wall farm kitchen ran the width of the house, and consisted of painted base cabinets with large curtained windows and open shelving above. The hardwood floor was dark with age, but scattered with pretty rugs. Antique kitchen implements were displayed on a pegboard over a massive six-burner stove. Alex saw strings of dried beans, peppers, and onions tacked along the wooden staircase leading up, and beneath it, opposite the work area, two long pine tables with matching benches met end to end.

Christina lowered her rather cumbersome body on to one of the benches and propped up swollen feet with a sigh. Meg placed a huge head of cabbage and a metal grater in front of her. 'Here you are, dear, a sit-down job in honour of your condition. And enjoy it while you can. Once the baby comes you'll forget what it's like to sit, sleep, or otherwise rest for at least six months.'

'Don't I know it,' Chris groaned, and was soon regaling Alex with tales of her first two pregnancies. 'You didn't meet my oldest,' she explained, 'but only because I couldn't pry him away from the barn and the pet goat his grandma lets him have.'

Her bright talk required only an occasional nod for response, and over the task of scraping carrots for the coleslaw Alex let a separate part of her mind wander. She enjoyed observing the McGee females in action, and noticed that they each had a definite role. Chris, the self-proclaimed chatterbox, kept a conversation going, while Laura and Meg, obviously the veterans of this kitchen, functioned side by side with smooth teamwork.

Caroline, on the other hand, was plainly the newcomer, and seemed more comfortable skirting the edges. Alex saw her folding the napkins, sorting the silverware, emptying ice trays, efficiently taking care of all the little details and at the same time staying out of the way.

'Tell us about yourself,' someone urged after a while, and Alex obligingly imparted a few details about her life and friends in Louisville.

'How did you get to know Jay?'

'Actually, we've just met.' She wondered what they would think about the true circumstances? She felt her face going warm... a reaction she hoped they would attribute to her vigorous scraping of the last carrot. 'He came up to the cabin to check my flue this morning,' she edited madly, 'and I suppose he invited me to dinner tonight because he thought I'd like to meet some of the people who knew my birth father.'

The conversation inevitably turned to Ty, and there was no mistaking the genuine fondness this family held for the man. Their memories of her father added more brush strokes to the portrait Kate and Jay had begun.

'You have his eyes,' Laura observed softly when the talk had ebbed. 'But you're like your mother in many ways. She was just about your age when I met her... blonde and petite, and much too fragile-looking to take on a new husband and a new way of life. Kate told me about the accident, Alex. I'm so sorry.'

Alex wiped carrot scrapings from the table. 'Thank you,' she managed to say thinly. 'I miss her... now more than ever. There are so many things I don't know.'

'About Ty?' Laura deduced. 'Maybe I can help.'

Alex glanced up, meaning to decline the offer, but found Laura's black eyes so compassionate that she confessed softly instead, 'I'd like to hear how they met.'

'Elise once told me that story, Alex. They were taking a college English course together, and the professor was so impressed with a paper Ty had written that he asked him to read it aloud. Ty, of course, was completely backward about things like that. He stumbled through a line or two, then froze. Elise felt sorry for him, took the paper and finished reading it. Ty swallowed his shyness long enough to invite her for coffee after class. From that day on they were inseparable.'

Alex felt an unexpected stricture in her throat. The idea of her father attending college didn't fit. 'I didn't realise he was an educated man.'

'Ty started school on a full academic scholarship,' Laura told her. 'But a few weeks into his second year a tractor rolled with his father and the old man was instantly killed. Ty had no choice afterwards but to come home and take over the farm. He brought Elise with him.'

'Just like that?'

Laura looked troubled. 'They were young. Eighteen, nineteen. I'm sure they had no idea what they were up against. For a while they lived with Ty's mother, your grandmother. She was bitter about the accident and resentful of the marriage, which hardly made things easier. Elise saw very little of Ty, and she didn't see her family at all. They made it plain from the start, you see, that Ty was not one of them... that he wouldn't be accepted. Perhaps if they'd taken the time to get to know him...' She trailed off. 'I'm sure they held a distorted view.'

Alex bit her lip, hearing her uncle's stiff voice again, feeling her stomach knot. 'The man was pure hayseed, Alex. He had dirt under his fingernails, filth on his boots. I can't tell you what Elise saw in him. She was a rebel in those days... maybe she enjoyed dragging the family down. At least she came to her senses and got out of the marriage before it was too late.'

Her involuntary wince drew Christina's hazel eyes and sympathy. 'It must have been quite a shock for you... Ty going like that. I mean, I know you hadn't seen him in years, but he was still your father.'

'I don't remember him.' A variation of the truth, at best, and enough to make her wonder what they really thought. That her mother had turned spiteful and kept Ty from seeing her? That he had unselfishly chosen not to complicate her new life? At least they didn't seem to share Jake's hard view of her character, and that small vote of confidence meant a lot. 'I wish he'd let me know he was ill.' Would she have come to meet him? Stayed and tried to get to know him? She wanted to believe so. She wanted them to believe so.

She leaned forward, a poignant question trembling on her lips, but before she could voice it, or even get a really firm grasp of it in her own mind, they heard a commotion in the next room, a burst of laughter and male voices raised in jest, and the mood was broken.

Distracted, Christina leaned her heavy body out and sideways until she could see into the living-room. 'It's Paula,' she informed them in an amused hiss. 'And she's kissing Jay to the back *teeth*.' She dangled there for a moment in morbid fascination, then muttered, 'Oops!' and popped upright again, face red.

The young woman who swept into the kitchen looked completely unrepentant. She held a cardboard box aloft. 'Jay's cake,' she explained brightly. 'Where shall I put it?'

Alex had never seen hair quite that shade, rich brown with a deep burgundy cast that was extremely attractive—and natural, as evidenced by the matching lashes that fringed her dark green eyes. A widow's peak at the wide forehead balanced out a delicate cleft chin. She's gorgeous, Alex thought with dismay. Drop-dead gorgeous.

'Sorry I'm late.' The girl deposited her box to the appointed counter-top, and offered Laura a peek inside. She stood, slim and enviably tall in a black jump suit, the long sleeves casually turned back and the tabbed waist encircled with the kind of belt that Alex could never carry off: wide, soft leather with a big mother-of-pearl clasp. 'I got a bit ambitious with the icing, and then— wouldn't you know it?—the Trans Am developed a knock, so I had to stop by the garage.'

'Nothing serious, I hope?' This came from Meg, and Alex wondered whether she'd imagined the tongue-in-cheek nuance.

'A chattering valve—you know Jake and his mechanic's vocabulary. But apparently it's no big deal.' Paula's clear green gaze travelled halfway about the room before falling on to Alex and widening. 'I didn't realise you had a guest, Laura.'

A final introduction revealed Paula Walker's place in the family: she was Caroline's sister. Alex felt obliged to peek into the box afterwards and murmur appreciative sounds with the others. It was a lovely cake, banked high with sugar roses, draped in curlicues and sprinkled with candy confetti. She had been served humbler cake at weddings, in fact, but swallowed down a perverse urge to say so.

'Paula's also an accomplished cook, seamstress, decorator, and housekeeper.'

'And don't forget matchmaker.'

Paula pulled a long-suffering face. 'Don't let them kid you, Alex. I'm the county extension agent, not Superwoman. And I certainly can't take credit for my sister's marriage, although I did introduce her to Josh when I moved to this post last spring. By the way——' her voice slid into a professional mode '—I hope you'll stop by the court-house if you need any help settling. I can give you a list of local businesses, suggest a nice place or two to eat. Even put you in touch with a good realtor.'

'I don't know how long I'm staying,' Alex declared with as much stubbornness as truth. She didn't care for Paula's assumption... which was absurd once she remembered that just yesterday she had been plotting the quickest route out of town.

Maybe Paula herself was the problem. Alex had experienced instant antagonism before, but this was unreasonable. By the time dinner graced the table she was gritting her teeth over Paula's finesse. Were the men really going to appreciate tiny scoops of margarine in a cut-glass dish? She resented her height, and her perfect face, and her gorgeous hair. But most of all she resented the thought of Paula kissing Jay to the back teeth. Alex hadn't even seen his back teeth, let alone kissed them.

She was therefore less than enthused to find Paula seated on Jay's other side—especially when everyone joined hands for John's moving, short grace, a tradition that Alex might have appreciated under different circumstances. Friendly chaos exploded seconds thereafter, and Alex sat drinking in the family's closeness yet feeling decidedly awkward among them, a sensation only heightened by Paula's obvious ease. Whether gossiping with the women, scoffing at the men's corny jokes, or flirting with Jay, Paula's every action told Alex that she belonged.

So? Alex berated her own tacit withdrawal. Turn on a little light of your own.

She picked up signals of dismay, sympathy, and even encouragement from the other females, who were all in a quandary. Jay had invited Alex to dinner. Technically that made him her date for the evening, but, since there was no polite way of saying as much, Paula was left ignorant of the situation and therefore free to usurp at will.

And Paula was an excellent usurper. Alex saw little more than the back of Jay's head during the meal. To his credit he did try to draw her into the conversation a couple of times, but with limited success, since their talk consisted of names and places Alex knew nothing about.

The rest of the McGees, however, did their best to fill the gaps. By the time dessert was offered Alex had made some interesting discoveries. Meredith, for instance, was an active Four-H Club member and intended to enter her Hereford bull calf in the state fair. And Laura, who had become a teacher after her sons had grown up, had founded a programme to counsel troubled students and was now acting as mentor to counties organising similar programmes.

And Caroline had a brand-new baby sleeping in the other room.

'My first nephew!' Paula beamed from the side-counter, where she was fussing over the cake. She bore it, brilliantly lit, back to the table. 'Thirty-two and one to grow on. Make a wish, Jay!'

There were no gifts—impractical for a family this large—but the brothers kept a long-standing tradition by reading Jay's birthday cards, all humorous, aloud. One by one the McGee men took the floor, beginning with John's embellished version of an Irish toast, and culminating with Joshua's unabashed ode to bachelorhood, which he immediately refuted by planting a kiss on his pink-faced bride.

Josh was taking a bow and Caroline still blushing when John Shawn arrived from the garage.

He withdrew from his overall pocket the torn back of a beer carton which had been folded to look like a card and slid a sheepish grin towards Jay. 'Uncle Jake sent me to read this... he said you'd understand.'

The room buzzed with murmurs and laughter; their great expectations of brother Jake were not lost on Alex. Looking half amused, half resigned, Jay settled back in his chair. 'Better get it over with, John Shawn.'

'OK.' The boy grinned wider and shrugged. 'Here goes...

There was an itty-bitty from the city,
Who clawed when she thawed, like a kitty.
I gave her to Jay,
For his latest birthday.
All in all, she was small, but darned pretty.'

Alex's face burned as John Shawn's halting voice gave way to silence. She registered the intrigued faces round the table and her heart hardened into absolute loathing for Jay's poetic brother. How could he do such a thing?

Her eyes locked into Jay's, expecting a similar reaction, and to her horror she saw instead that he was fighting to keep that twitch of a grin from spreading across his mouth. He lost the battle and, worse, the grin erupted into bellows of laughter, drawing echoes from the other men.

'Well, Jay,' Laura smiled quizzically, 'is this something you care to explain to the rest of us?'

'I wouldn't attempt it.' He shook his head, still laughing. 'This is between Jake and me.'

'And Alex?' Paula asked in a significantly cool voice. She might not be privy to the details, but she had caught the main drift very well, thank you.

'Alex?' John Shawn had squeezed between Meredith and Scott on one of the benches, heaped his plate high and stuffed a forkful into his mouth before Paula drew attention to the dinner guest among the crowd. He ran a self-conscious hand over his head, where the shape of the oil-stained cap he'd tossed aside still lay on his hair like a helmet. His voice was muffled with both potatoes and consternation. 'Nobody told me you'd be here.'

'Never mind the way you look, John Shawn.' Meredith announced quite bluntly, 'Alex is Uncle Jay's date.'

Alex felt her cheeks grow even warmer. As Paula's accusing look gave way to disconcertedness she thought briefly of quipping 'Is this where we step outside together?' But good manners and an odd twinge of compassion kept her quiet. One of those painful three-second silences beset the room, punctuated only by a small gasp from Meredith as though someone had kicked her under the table. Then several voices rang out at once, overly jubilant, and the awkward moment passed.

Whether intentionally or not, Paula had her revenge.

They had finished coffee, cake, and a free-for-all with the dish-washing when Caroline brought her freshly wakened son out to the living-room. 'Here's a McGee you haven't met.' She stopped beside Alex's chair, her pretty face soft with maternal pride. 'Adam?' she crooned. 'Say hello to Alex, darling.'

Alex peered into the wrinkled small face and saw that the baby's fuzzy hair was indeed as light as her own, and that his scalp was palest pink beneath it, just as Jake McGee had said. 'Would you like to hold him?' Caroline offered, already putting the child into her arms. 'Just keep one hand behind his neck. He'll be fine.'

It shouldn't have been an ordeal to get Adam settled, yet Alex was both terrified and fascinated by the warm little bundle, and so extremely conscious of the experienced females surrounding her that she couldn't relax. To her alarm the baby's tiny head doddered all over her shoulder, face-first. 'He's just making his nest.' Caroline looked on lovingly. 'Getting comfortable,' she translated. 'He's fine.'

But no, he wasn't fine. A few more seconds of doddering, then he let out a lusty wail. Almost before Alex knew what was happening, the crying infant had been lifted from her arms, and Paula was cooing, 'Come to Auntie, darling,' as if she'd rescued him from ill-treatment. A few pats on the new-born's back made him snuggle close, then 'Auntie' spared a faint smile for Alex. 'Babies become nervous around a nervous adult, that's all. Don't let it bother you. Not all women are born with maternal instincts.'

But it did bother her, Alex reflected on the way home. The episode was a direct blow to her femininity... a new entry on the list of personal failures that haunted her: inept with babies and small children. Lacks maternal capabilities. Can't hold the attention of her date.

'Alex? I hope you aren't falling asleep on me?'

'No,' she turned her head along the seat back, rejecting the indulgence in Jay's husky voice, 'that's not on my list.'

He searched her face in the near-darkness, his smile slight, quizzical. 'Is something wrong?'

Did he really have to ask? First, he had abandoned her to a roomful of strangers, and then, while she'd been shaving the skins off more carrots than she could count, he had let himself be kissed to the back teeth... without struggle. But, worst of all, he'd left her in the position of having to compete for his attention. It had been humiliating and a flagrant violation of protocol, and she longed to tell him so. 'What could possibly be wrong?' she asked instead.

'The idea,' he quickly returned the volley, 'is for you to tell me.'

'Maybe I'd like to test your instincts.'

He caught her eyes again, frowning in the faint light of the dashboard. 'Fine... if that kind of game pleases you. Why don't we talk about Jake's poem?'

'*Limerick*,' she corrected irritably. 'And tonight was my first time starring in one. I didn't enjoy it. I found it... demeaning.'

'It wasn't meant to be.'

Her jaw tensed. 'So it was just your brother's way of showing how much he *likes* me. That's why you busted a gut laughing.'

'*Alex*.' Jay sounded both amused and exasperated. 'You've got this completely wrong. The poem wasn't meant to insult you, honey. In fact, it wasn't meant for you at all.'

'Come on, Jay! "From the city", "itty-bitty",' she quoted in a scathing tone. 'Of course it was meant for me.'

'OK, it was *about* you, but you're missing my point.' His pause took on a distinctly apologetic flavour. 'Jake wrote the damned thing for Paula.'

'*Paula?*' Alex breathed. 'Jay, you're as crazy as he is, and even crazier than I am, and that's the craziest——' She abandoned her tirade to stare. 'What are you doing?'

'Pulling off the road,' he stated the obvious as a feathery pine bough scraped softly against the hood of the truck. 'I can see you're going to need some background information before you can appreciate my brother's little joke.'

'I've had it up to here——' Alex sliced a hand across her throat '——with Jake's little jokes, and I really don't see what——'

'Alex, please.' He pressed a finger to her mouth. 'Just listen; it will take a minute.' The unexpected touch silenced her and he let his hand drop. 'Now. Maybe Paula told you that this time last year she was new in town? Well, new ladies in town being scarce, Jake and I both took her out for a while. You could even say that the competition got fairly...heated.'

'Oh, great. A triangle.'

Jay swore mildly under his breath. 'I was talking about last year, remember? What I'm trying to tell you is that Paula and I have since come to an understanding. She's my brother's girl. End of story.'

'Maybe she should read the story again,' Alex flared, then backtracked. 'I mean...she didn't act much like Jake's girl.'

'Paula likes to flirt.' Jay shrugged. 'She enjoys being outrageous. And she likes seeing the family speculate. It's harmless fun, and, I suspect, a way of retaliating to Jake's wild streak.'

'I see.' Alex glowered at the frosty purple darkness. Was Jay really as unconcerned as he appeared? 'So where does the poem fit in?'

'Think about it. Paula appears at Jake's station, dressed to kill, showing off this fantastic cake...my cake...and one hour later John Shawn arrives with a note scribbled on a scrap of cardboard. Does that sound like coincidence? Do you think Jake left himself shorthanded on the busiest night of the week just to get a laugh?'

'I think he picked a lousy way to make Paula jealous, if that's what you're suggesting. All he did was insult me.'

'Oh, I thought a certain grudging admiration shone through.'

Alex pulled a face. 'I suppose Jake has a few admirable qualities of his own...'

'Just ask Paula,' Jay suggested neatly. 'She'll tell you that my brother is a great guy who needs a swift kick. The man is thirty-six, in love for the first time, and it scares the hell out of him.'

'So tonight—the cake and all—was just a bluff. Paula used you for leverage the way Jake used me in his poem.'

Chewing her lip, Alex squinted into the lights of an oncoming car. When it had passed she told him haltingly, 'I'd hate to think I was part of some...*situation* the three of you have going. If that's all this evening was about then don't let's repeat it. My life is complicated enough.'

There was no immediate reaction. After a moment she looked at Jay and found him frowning incredulously. 'Do you actually believe I'd do that?'

'I don't know what you might do. When it comes down to the wire we only met this morning——'

'Last night.'

'All right, last night, and, while you've been very sweet to me,' she continued in a fierce little rush, 'I'd have to be an idiot not to wonder why. So I'm just saying, now, that if this...thing between Paula and your brother might be the reason, I want out.'

'What if it had nothing to do with them?' Jay challenged half angrily. The air in the Blazer was suddenly super-charged with tension; Alex felt her pulse stir accordingly, and her mouth go dry. 'What if I had a more conventional reason?' He reached out to tuck a strand of hair behind her ear, the gesture so innocent that it was seductive. 'The *only* reason?' he stressed darkly. 'Would you still want out?'

Alex swallowed. 'I...I don't know what you mean.'

His hand wandered to the nape of her neck, massaging, sliding up to wind itself in the warmth of her hair. 'I think you do.' With slow, almost frightening deliberation he drew her very close. 'As a matter of fact, I'm sure you do.' He stared into her eyes, the look searching and unmistakably heated. Then he kissed her.

Alex fought to control her reaction. She had been kissed before. She should be able to respond without her body quivering like this. But it was impossible not to quiver for Jay. He had the softest kiss imaginable, and then, just when she thought her mouth would simply melt and fuse beneath his with sheer longing, he hardened the pressure into something altogether different...

That odd little moan could not have come from her. Her head was somehow lying on Jay's chest, and it felt muzzy, as if she needed to be sent to the decompression chamber. Dark, tender amusement shone from his eyes. 'Are you OK?'

'Yes, and no,' she murmured wryly. 'I didn't expect that.'

'And I didn't plan it.' Jay drew a slow fingertip across her mouth. 'But tell a man he's *sweet* and all hell breaks loose. I don't feel very sweet right now.'

'That's funny——' with an almost juvenile self-consciousness she rubbed her face against his shoulder '—you feel fine to me.'

Jay's soft laugh wounded her. 'Alex, I'm trying to apologise here.'

'Don't you dare.' She sat up, no longer quite so enchanted, and gave him a guarded look. 'You didn't *compromise* me, Jay. It was just a kiss.'

'You sure know how to deflate a man's ego.' When his dry grin received no response he chided, 'And don't look at me that way. I *should* be sorry.'

'Why?' Alex demanded coolly. 'Weren't you enjoying yourself?'

'Maybe too much.' A shadow of a grin played briefly across his mouth. Then he sighed and slid an arm around her shoulders, his fingers sifting idly through her tumbled hair. 'My dad once told me,' he related huskily, 'that getting to know a woman is like reading a book. The cover attracts you, right? So you open it up and you scan a few pages. Then if you're still interested you start reading. At that point one of three things is bound to happen: either you'll lose interest and stop; you'll get impatient and skip ahead to the exciting parts; or else you'll take your time...' he paused to brush a gentle kiss atop her head '...and savour every passage, because the story is just too good to be rushed.'

He tipped her face up, his eyes warm. 'My dad was a wise man, honey. I don't want to rush anything with you.'

He kissed her once more, briefly, and then turned the key in the ignition to signal the end of their dalliance. Alex shakily moved back to her own seat as he put the truck in gear. Perhaps it was for the best that he had backed off. She needed to stop and think. Recoup some perspective.

Not that she had any trouble tagging Jay's book parable for a smooth line. She was a smart girl. She realised that day-old relationships could not support that depth of feeling. She just wanted to believe that he meant it. With everything in her she wanted to believe. Heart fluttering wildly, she leaned her head against the seat back and stared at one brilliant star hanging in the purple sky. Feeling this happy terrified her.

CHAPTER FIVE

Two hours later Alex still lay awake, every muscle in her body rigid. Having resolutely turned out the lights, she was trying not to notice how the fire behind various little cracks and chinks in the wood stove lent a weird reddish glow to the room.

Ty's winter coat had been the only thing heavy enough to replace the wet quilt as cover; it was warm and her toes stayed tightly curled beneath it. Yet from time to time she shivered, too fraught to straighten the nightgown that had twisted uncomfortably about her legs.

Was it like this for her mother? she wondered. Did Elise ever lie in this bed, in this room, staring at the ceiling because she couldn't sleep, feeling alien and alone in this place... in this town full of strangers?

And what about him? Was he really the wonderful, gentle, thoughtful man they kept describing? Or was he the hick Uncle Stuart had told her about? Just one more stranger and a tragic mistake?

By the Bannons' standards, Elise had married far beneath her station in life. Had that been part of the attraction? Had she fallen in love with Ty because he'd been so different from the country club members' sons who had filled her social calendar? Had she abandoned him for the very same reason?

Full of unanswered questions and feeling desperate, Alex got out of bed and peered through the window, into the dark veil of trees. Jay's light was out, just as it had been out the last time she'd looked... when she'd discovered her tranquillisers were missing. Darn it, Jay.

She crawled back under the sheet and coat, too proud to wake him in the middle of the night for a sleeping pill. *Why couldn't you mind your own business? Why did you have to be so concerned?*

Even though the mental gripe made her feel better, a part of her contrarily acknowledged that she loved the way Jay McGee had involved himself with her. She also found a distinct sense of comfort in having him near. It was like renting a great apartment within a few blocks of the police station. Help was only minutes away.

But when did help become a priority? she mused disparagingly with her next breath. *Where is Oliver Wendell Bannon's independent granddaughter now? What became of the confident girl who once inhabited this body? There's nothing noble left in me,* she thought, with wide eyes focused damply on the ceiling. *It's only a matter of time before Jay sees that.*

She drew one slender arm free... on top of the coat to idly stroke the scratchy material with her fingertips.

Was *he* anything like Jay? she wondered. Was he gentle and sensitive, and completely natural to be around?

The outdoorsy scent of pine needles and wood smoke and some other elusive ingredient filled her nostrils. Alex ran both hands over the rough tweedy cloth, fingering the welt seams and worn buttons before moving on to the deep pockets, one of which contained a conspicuous bulge. Her left hand closed on a small object, unidentifiable by touch alone. Slowly, curiously, she drew it out.

A pipe lay in her hand, its round, polished bowl tapped clean. Alex brought it close to her face to sniff the lingering tobacco smell. Before she could register its familiarity or even brace herself the scent had triggered a mind image so vivid that it frightened her.

From some deep well of memory she heard her own childish chuckles as a nest of blue smoke rings hovered just beyond her reach. Face upturned, she strained with all her might to catch them. But the rings eluded her tiny hands and dissolved untouched against the ceiling. *This* ceiling.

Gasping in shock, Alex flung the pipe across the room.

The next moment she was flinging the bedclothes aside to scramble after it. She examined the smooth wood bowl for cracks, then cradled it protectively in both hands when she found none. Trembling, she crawled back into bed.

What was happening to her?

Night-time had a way of magnifying emotions. Alex didn't know whether to attribute this to a basic human distrust of darkness, or simply to the heightened concentration that stemmed from still silence. She only knew that she was relieved to see daylight filtering through her uncurtained windows. She felt better making the bed than huddling in it. She needed to *do* something.

Morning gave her plenty to do. There was no automatic drip coffee-maker here. She had to coax fresh fire from a few glowing coals in the wood stove before she could even think about coffee. Then the old-fashioned enamel pot took forever to boil, perhaps because she was watching it. She had pulled a kitchen chair close to the stove, not out of impatience, but purely in her quest for warmth, and she still had her father's old coat clutched around her.

The pipe was there in her hand. Morning dulled both menace and magic, pushing a sense of acute puzzlement to the foreground. Alex studied the small round bowl of it and the short ivory-tipped stem, and tried to recall anyone in her past who might have smoked a pipe. She reasoned that it didn't have to be this *particular* pipe which had triggered last night's flash of memory. How *could* it have been, in fact? As Jay had pointed out yesterday, ten-month-old babies didn't store that kind of memory...at least not on any accessible level. The trouble was, she couldn't come up with anyone else. Robert had smoked a rare after-dinner cigar, Grandfather hadn't smoked at all, and there had been few other men in her childhood.

There was something else bothering her, too...something that Alex hated admitting even to herself. But, as unsettling as the first scent of that pipe had been, the smell and the feel of the old coat was equally and oppositely...*comforting*.

And why not? Alex reasoned in an effort to marshal her runaway thoughts. This coat had been keeping her warm all night.

As if to prove the point she cast it off and rose, shivering, to pour coffee. The brew was horribly bitter, but she drank it anyway, needing the caffeine to coax her weary body through the motions of washing and dressing and making-up.

But the concealer had not done its job, she reflected half an hour later. Grey shadows ringed her eyes, and, in spite of her liberal use of blusher, she looked wan. Nor did her beige fisherman's sweater help the situation. She was in the process of exchanging it for a soft pink one when she heard a knock on the door and realised that she stood neatly framed by the uncovered front window. She was going to have to do something about curtains.

She hastily settled the pink cashmere over her head and adjusted its fluffy turned-down neck. If she'd wanted more colour in her face then she had indeed got her wish. She could feel her cheeks growing warmer by the minute. The *source* of that warmth, however, was not lying against her skin but rather standing on her front porch!

Jay looked so good wearing a pale blue dress shirt with grey trousers and his leather jacket that Alex almost lost track of her embarrassment. Almost. 'Oh. Good morning, Jay.' It was hard to appear nonchalant when he had probably seen her half-naked torso—again.

His lop-sided grin spoke for itself. 'I seem to have a lousy sense of timing. Sorry.'

'It's OK.' Alex fidgeted nervously with the hem of her sweater. 'My fault for not putting the curtains back up, but I'm thinking of getting new ones so I didn't waste the time.' She was prattling. 'You look nice this morning.' She forced a note of confidence into her voice. A cool gust of wind blasted them, and she hastily drew Jay inside. 'Are you going somewhere special?'

'Um-hmm. Church.' Hands in pockets, he stood near the closed door. 'Would you like to come with me? It's short notice, but I didn't think to ask last night.'

If her blush had been receding a bit, thoughts of last night revived it. 'Thanks,' Alex forced her mind back to the point, 'but I've never been a particularly religious person. I mean, I believe what I believe, but as far as taking part in any organisation I——'

'You don't have to justify yourself to me,' Jay interrupted mildly. 'It was just an invitation.'

'I suppose it took me by surprise.' She chewed on her lip. 'You don't seem the type.'

He quirked a brow. 'The type to go to church?'

'Well...'

Jay grinned faintly at her discomfiture. 'You can't pen people into *types*, Alex. They'll jump the fence every time.'

Maybe it was the knowledge that she'd spent half the night trying to pigeonhole Ty Conway that made her voice sound so jerky. 'I concede. Would you like some coffee?'

'Sure, thanks.'

'I should warn you, it's not very good.' She crossed to the big cast-iron sink that served as both draining-board and counter-top, and took two cups from the metal cabinet overhead. They were made of serviceable white pottery, one chipped, the other cracked. 'Until this morning I'd never tried making coffee on top of the stove.' She found a pot-holder and poured. 'Have a seat, Jay. Do you take cream and sugar?'

'No. Black's fine.' He pulled up a kitchen chair and reached almost immediately for the pipe she'd left there, turning it slowly in his hands. Alex slipped into her own chair and pushed Jay's cup across. He sipped and swallowed, but made no comment.

'Bitter, isn't it?' she said distractedly. She was much more interested in what he thought of the pipe than what he thought of her coffee.

'There's a trick for that,' Jay told her. 'Drop an eggshell in the pot next time.'

Alex drank and pulled a face. 'Aren't *you* a wealth of information?'

'Just practical stuff.' He was still holding the pipe, the pad of one thumb idly stroking satin wood. 'I've been absorbing it since I was a baby.'

Drawing unexpected courage from that comment, Alex focused on the object in his hand. 'I found that in Ty's coat pocket last night.' Her tone was too offhand... too falsely bright. 'The tobacco smells nice, don't you think?'

Jay's eyes caught her and she knew that he had seen the way her fingers trembled round her cup. 'Yes, I do.'

Alex took another sip of coffee, wishing she hadn't started this, wondering what it was that she expected from Jay... some revelation? Ty's pipe had preoccupied him from the moment he had seen it, just as it had dominated her own thoughts for the better part of last night, and she found herself longing... hoping... for an answer.

She was tempted to tell him about the memory. The vision, or *whatever* it was, that had upset her. Yet the fact that she couldn't describe it in her own mind left her reluctant to make the verbal effort. Suppose he thought, as she halfway feared herself, that she was cracking up...imagining something that hadn't happened? 'You're smiling,' she finally commented.

Jay's faint smile tugged into a reminiscent grin. 'I was just remembering how this pipe fascinated me as a kid. Ty could blow the most amazing smoke rings!'

Alex's face suddenly felt as if it were covered in clay mask, and cracking. 'Did they hover inside one another,' she asked carefully, 'then spiral apart?'

'Exactly.' Jay's brow shot up. 'How did you know?'

'You tell me!' Her voice shook with strain. 'I...oh, Jay.' She pressed a hand to her forehead. 'This is so *weird*.'

'Alex, look at me.' She obeyed and saw his eyes darken with concern. 'You're trembling. What's going on?'

'That's just it.' She made a futile little wave. 'I don't *know* what's going on. I was lying in bed last night, thinking about my mother...and him. I had his coat thrown over me, and somehow the feel and the smell of it just seemed so...familiar. Then I pushed my hands into the pockets and found the pipe, and suddenly I could see those smoke rings in my mind and hear myself laughing—the way a child laughs—and grabbing at them. And don't tell me it didn't happen, Jay. The details might be a little hazy, but the sensation was real.'

'Alex——'

'I know,' she interrupted, disgusted with herself for having told him, angry because he didn't believe her, 'babies don't remember. I know that! Why do you think I'm so shaken up?'

He reached across the table to take her hand, which was now clenched into a tight fist. 'Is it possible you dreamed it?'

'Another coincidence?' she scoffed, impatient. 'How? You said yourself his smoke rings were amazing. And besides that,' she added her *coup de grâce*, 'I haven't slept.'

'Your pills,' Jay deduced emotionlessly. He leaned back to delve a slow hand into his shirt pocket. 'I found them on the kitchen counter this morning. I had hoped you were able to rest without them.'

'If I could rest without them I wouldn't be taking them.'

He frowned a little. 'Couldn't your doctor suggest an alternative method?'

'Sure. Counting sheep,' Alex ticked off, 'relaxation exercises, meditation, camomile tea, and warm milk. I've tried them all,' she admitted in a weary voice. 'Believe me, Jay. Nothing works.'

'You do realise that these things can become addictive?'

'Yes,' she said shortly. 'But they're the lesser of two evils at this point... I'm sorry if my weakness offends you.'

'It's none of my business——'

'No, it's none of your business.'

'—but,' Jay went on huskily, 'as crazy as this might sound after only two days, I care what happens to you.' He stared at her, and Alex thought with a kind of self-betrayal that he had the warmest, gentlest, sexiest eyes she'd ever seen. 'You look so exhausted, baby.'

'Oh, please don't,' she got out raggedly, propping chin in hand. 'Don't be nice to me. If you're nice to me I swear I'll cry.'

'Would that be the worst thing in the world?' he asked in a reasonable tone. Scraping his chair back from the table, Jay patted his thigh. 'Why don't you come over here?'

Alex swallowed and straightened up, but her eyes were still brimming. 'I'm not a child, Jay.'

'You don't have to convince me of that.' A suggestive smile hovered for a moment, then disappeared. 'But it's nice to be treated like a child sometimes, isn't it? All I want is to hold you.'

'Why?' she asked numbly, conscious of very little now except the urge to slide over there into his arms.

Jay sighed. 'Because I like you,' he told her with exaggerated simplicity. 'Now will you come over here?'

Alex went.

'I'll bet,' she mused some time later with the thud of his heart directly beneath her ear, 'that I'm the first girl who ever sat on your lap and didn't tickle your chin with her hair.'

'Um-hmm,' he agreed, 'if you don't count my nieces.'

'On the other hand,' Alex reasoned, 'it would be hard, even for a tall person, to tickle a chin covered with so much beard.' She stretched up a palm to slowly stroke the thick, trimmed whiskers, feeling oddly free to say anything that came into her head. 'Uhm, that feels nice,' she murmured in a languid tone. 'What made you grow a beard?'

He laughed. 'All good professors have beards, Alex.'

'I never sat on a professor's knee before,' she said, then added cheekily, 'but I made straight As in college anyway.' Jay was rocking them very slowly back and forth on the chair's rear legs, and, if she'd felt a little ridiculous about that at first, she was now getting used to it. Her head was as light as a dandelion puff. 'Do you think that's where the word "scatter-brain" came from?' she mused. 'Dandelions?' When Jay chuckled again the sound seemed far away. She tried to open her eyes, but it took too much effort. 'What are you trying to do,' she accused softly, 'put me to sleep?'

'Is it working?' he asked, the smile there in his voice.

Alex moved her blonde head against his chest, too exhausted even to be amazed. 'Yes,' she sighed, 'I think it is.'

Alex's wrists ached from wringing water out of the thick quilt, and she staggered beneath the weight of it as she arranged the sodden folds over a clothes-line strung in the back yard. She was whistling a tuneless little song beneath her breath. The sunshine on her face felt wonderful.

She had stirred only minutes before to find herself lying on the bed, covered with the old coat, and unable to remember a thing about getting there. The fire was out, but the day had warmed to compensate, sunlight streaming in everywhere. *Afternoon* sunlight, she realised with a quick glance at her watch. She'd only slept a few hours, but it felt like eight.

She gave the quilt one last tug and pat, then stood with both hands pressed in the small of her back to survey the narrow yard. There was an old boarded-up well with honeysuckle vines growing around it, a row of chicken coops, all clean and empty, and the shed. Beyond that was thick wooded hillside. Steep hillside, Alex noticed, with a hand shielding her eyes. At the very tip-top she saw a ledge of sheer rock.

'Feel like taking a walk?'

She hadn't heard Jay's approach. 'Up there?' She whirled in some confusion, a collection of unrelated thoughts running through her head: that he had changed from church clothes into jeans and a warm shirt; that his eyes were all golden and crinkled at the corners; that she felt vulnerable. 'Wouldn't that be a little ambitious?'

'We'd never make it to the cliff and back before dark. But if you're interested we can tour the rest of Ty's place. *Alex's* place,' he corrected himself. 'Spend the afternoon with me?'

For a while they walked about, inspecting the outbuildings and the yard, discussing one thing or another that needed to be done, as if Alex planned on staying indefinitely instead of just the month. They had worked their way to the front of the house when Jay frowned and went down on his haunches to inspect a dormant vine near the porch. 'This needs to go.'

'But I like honeysuckle.'

'You won't like it nearly so much when it destroys your front steps.'

Alex gave a small, wistful shrug and, when he began to dig up the vine with his pocket knife, turned towards the yard. 'These dogwoods look like stair-steps,' she commented presently of the grove of trees. 'Each one is a little shorter than the last.'

'That's because Ty only planted one a year. Always on September twenty-first.' Distracted by his task, Jay did not see Alex pale. 'He never said what made that date significant.'

'Maybe I can tell you,' Alex offered thinly. She felt shaken and unexpectedly burdened by her father's touching gesture, yet what other explanation could there be? 'September twenty-first,' she said in a strained voice, 'is my birthday.'

Jay slowly folded his knife away, his eyes compassionate on her tense face. He said nothing, giving her time, she supposed, to cope, and after a moment she dashed a hand across her eyes and, staring forward, said half-heartedly, 'The cabin's very old, isn't it?'

'Your great-great-grandfather Ezekiel Conway built it.' Jay easily picked up the change of subject. 'He cut the logs himself and dragged them out of the woods with a mule. Then he hauled chimney stone by wagon——'

'No offence to Great-Great-Grandfather Conway,' Alex interrupted huskily, 'but why didn't he build a real fireplace?'

'Because in those days anybody could have a fireplace. A wood stove was a luxury.'

'Like the pull-chain toilet and the water pump?'

'The pull-chain didn't come until later.' Jay grinned faintly. 'But there's an interesting story about the well. Ever hear of a water witch, Alex?'

'A what?'

'Water witch. Your great-great-grandfather is reputed to have been one, meaning that he could find buried water with a peach-tree limb. Not only did he divine the location of his own well——' he gestured towards the vine-covered box '—but he was so famous for pinpointing underground springs that folks came from ten counties to hire his talents.'

Alex blinked, expecting him to laugh at any minute. He had to be pulling her leg. 'So how did he do it?' she prompted.

'He'd walk along slowly with one fork of a split limb held loosely in each hand and the main branch pointing ahead. When the limb turned downward he'd found water.'

'I see.' Tongue-in-cheek, Alex asked, 'I suppose water witching is strictly an ancient art?'

'A dying one, anyway. My brother Josh has done it, although he prefers a length of copper rod to the peach tree limb, and he'll be the first to tell you that a modern drilling company is just as reliable.' Jay cocked a brow. 'You aren't buying any of this, are you?'

'None.'

'Then it won't do any good to tell you that Josh is the seventh son of a seventh son, and endowed with special powers.'

'Such as?'

'An understanding of herbs, the ability to stop bleeding... healing powers.'

'Ah.' Feeling better, Alex tilted back her head. Her hair swung and settled with the movement, so pale that it seemed opalescent in sunlight. 'And what about the fifth son, Jay? What special powers do you possess?'

'Apparently not the gift of convincing folklore.' He stood smiling down at her for a time, his eyes thoughtful...almost intense. Then he shook his head slightly as if to clear it. 'Let me at least prove myself as a historian,' he challenged softly. 'Ready for that walk?'

They hiked for perhaps half a mile into the woods, Alex shuffling through decomposed leaves and fallen pine needles with a reckless disregard for her cream leather boots. A regular runner, she had no trouble making the steep incline behind Jay. It was looking down again that left her breathless. 'I thought we weren't going to the cliff today.'

'We aren't,' Jay turned to assure her. 'As a matter of fact, we're here.'

'Oh, good,' Alex sighed. She suddenly felt far more winded by him than by the mountain. A strong and unpredictable force was sex appeal; after following Jay's broad back for what seemed like ages she was besieged by a desire to just look at him...as if here in this rustic and secluded setting his considerable male power had become doubly potent.

She averted her eyes within seconds, however, the need to guard her feelings surpassing any need to indulge them.

'This is an unusual place,' she commented. They were standing near the base of yet another ridge, this one surely insurmountable...unless Jay meant to lead her over a rock pile and up a gully filled with rotting leaves and twigs. Trees rose on all sides...bare maples and poplars, white-trunked beeches, massive chestnuts and walnuts, assorted evergreens. A small animal's scurry broke the quiet—probably a squirrel. Earlier a grown rabbit had leapt from the bushy undergrowth to nearly frighten Alex to death, but at least, or so Jay had promised, there were no snakes.

He intercepted another nervous glance and guessed the reason for it, his husky laugh breaking her tension. 'What a babe in the woods! Look, even if the snakes were out of hibernation, chances are you wouldn't see one. They prefer to hide under fallen logs, or low bushes, or——' he pointed to a spot further along '—in places like that.'

Alex peered in the direction he'd indicated, gradually realising that what she'd dismissed as an outcrop of rock was not a natural formation at all, rather man-made. Only five feet now at its highest point and badly crumbled, the wall had once spanned the deep gully. Upon closer inspection she noted that its remains and foundation consisted entirely of irregularly shaped stones, pieced together with considerable skill to form a barricade.

Alex had read of primitive Indian sites scattered statewide; she knew enough to recognise this as one of them. Excitement glowing deep in her eyes, she asked softly, 'How old is it?'

Jay stepped up behind her, hands cupping her shoulders, arms enfolding her body as she automatically moved backwards to meet him. 'This particular fortification dates to about 1200 AD,' he said, 'but some in the state are much older. It was built by the inhabitants of a small dwelling village once located near the base of the cliff.' He pointed out a spot high above them. 'See where the ridge flattens? That semicircle of land was ideal for camping and corn planting. Water was no problem...it ran right out of the ground. Add the natural advantage of being able to look down on one's enemies, and you have a prime location. One the prehistoric Indian found worth protecting.' He went on to tell her about the village people...skilled hunters and tool-makers, simple agriculturists, utilitarian potters. Alex's imagination swiftly took hold as he talked, bombarding her with poignant images, making her shiver. 'Cold?' Jay's hold tightened.

'No...just a little overwhelmed.' She stood silent in Jay's arms for long moments before attempting to further express herself, and then it didn't really translate. 'I was thinking about the people who lived and worked and bore children, and even lost their lives right here. To stand on the same ground is...' she cast about for the proper word '...*humbling*.'

'Places like this do put time in perspective,' Jay agreed. 'One day it will be our possessions in the glass cases, and our lives in the history books.' He rested his chin lightly atop her head. 'Future kids will pretend to be twentieth-century heroes the way I once played Indian warrior.'

Alex's thoughtful expression gave way to a smile. She was picturing the young Jay with bow and arrow and feathers. 'Tell me,' she impulsively slid a hand into one of his, 'did you ever play here?'

'Sure.' Jay tangled their fingers together. 'It was a long way from home, but worth the walk. My brothers and I staged some pretty fantastic battles along these bluffs.'

She pulled a wry face. 'I suppose Jake led the invaders?'

'Like a true savage,' Jay laughed. 'With skill, cunning, and no mercy.'

Alex could well imagine. But beyond enjoying a joke at Jake McGee's expense she had no intention of letting him intrude. 'You have to admire the early man's defence tactics,' she commented presently. 'By blocking the only passage up this ridge he'd secured the south-west half of the area. The cliff formed a natural barrier to the east.' She narrowed her eyes in concentration. 'What about the north side?'

'His weakest point,' Jay acknowledged. 'Any invasion probably came from a narrow north slope... where the main barricade was erected.'

'I'd love to see it.' Alex twisted around, eyes eager. 'How do we get there—the gully?'

'Or else we hike around the perimeter—but I'm afraid you'd be disappointed. By the time old Ezekiel had built his chimney, shored up his well, and played benevolent neighbour to the whole mountainside there wasn't much left.'

Alex was stunned. 'You mean he robbed stone from these walls?'

'The land did belong to him.' Jay tempered her reaction. 'And bear in mind that our ancestors were a practical people—they had to be. Why expend valuable time on a task the prehistoric Indian had already done? Although I'm sure Zeke and his friends were duly impressed by the work. To offer any protection the original barricades had to be at least ten feet high—that's a lot of rock. And when you consider the weight of some of them, and the distance they were moved... from the creek or river-bed, or the mountain-top, you have to appreciate the early man's perseverance. Ezekiel had his hands full just getting the rock out again.'

Alex stared at the crumbled wall, a peculiar hollowness in her stomach. 'How could he destroy something so important?'

'You sound like your father talking.' Jay smiled faintly. 'Once this property came into Ty's hands it was holy ground. He felt very strongly about such places... they could be enjoyed, but not disturbed.'

'Yet he let seven boys tramp over the fort?'

'Only with the understanding that we'd respect the site... a bargain not so easily kept when all we could think about was secret caves and hidden treasure. Ty allowed us to keep anything we found on the surface, but the area had been picked virtually clean already. Over time, the points and bone needles that I collected started to seem like no big deal. What I really wanted to do was dig.

'I was seventeen or so when temptation finally got the better of me.' He stood looking towards the bluff, face impassive. 'I smuggled a shovel up there and excavated one of the small mounds.'

Alex knew that most Indian mounds were mortuary, but, even having seen Jay's magnificent collection of relics, the possibility that he would go to such lengths in acquiring them had not occurred to her. Nor was she prepared for her own reaction. Barely suppressing a note of censure, she asked, 'What did you find?'

'A man's skeleton,' he told her after a moment. 'He had been buried with an axe on his chest and a spear by his side. Around him there were scrapers, arrowheads, pottery... everything he might need in the afterlife.'

Alex hesitated, unsure what to say. Jay had been young, after all, when it had happened... an overly curious boy who had done something forbidden. But his matter-of-fact tone chilled her. 'Did you keep any of those things?'

'No. My brother Joe had seen me take the shovel. He put two and two together and, being younger, smaller, and——' he grimaced '—probably smarter than me, chose to warn Ty. They arrived before I'd touched anything. Ty stood over me while I replaced every cubic inch of earth... I don't think I'd ever seen him so angry. To make a long, painful story short, he swore that I'd never set foot on his land again.'

And yet here you are, Alex thought. Does that mean there was a reconciliation? Did he relent afterwards... my father? Some important premise seemed to flash in and out of her head...too fast for comprehension. 'Did he change his mind?'

'About the digging? No, never. Not that it made any difference,' Jay added softly. 'That ancient warrior had already taken his hold.

'I grew up with old campsites...rock houses...burial mounds all around me, but that was the day I became *aware* of them.' He narrowed his eyes at some far-away point. 'For better or worse, I was hooked.'

That elusive thought flashed through again. Alex shifted slowly from one foot to the other, and in doing so put distance between herself and Jay. Her stomach began steadily knotting...like the rope of a child's spinning swing, and a peculiar coldness enveloped her. Seeds of suspicion matured and spread roots. But her work as an interviewer had taught her the value of neutrality...at least until she got her story. Voice level, she asked, 'What did you do?'

Jay turned, studying her face, frowning at its lack of expression. 'I joined the university's archaeology programme, and eventually took part in several digs. There were a few glory days...I won't kid you. But there were countless more days when we sifted nothing but pottery shards and fish bones from some overworked midden and frustration ate away at my gut because I knew of a dozen untouched sites...sites that would make a real difference to what we were trying to do. I even brought one of my professors back here with an impassioned speech for Ty about the wealth of scientific knowledge laying waste in those mounds——'

'Which he resisted?'

'Which he resisted,' Jay confirmed, 'with threats of buckshot thrown in for good measure.'

Alex did not respond to his faint smile. 'But if the opportunity arose,' she conjectured carefully, 'I imagine you could find support for the effort. That is, if the site still interests you?'

'The new laws prohibit unauthorised digging.' His slow, searching gaze nearly unnerved her. 'And I'm not an archaeologist. I gave it up to teach. Remember?'

'But you are a collector,' she stressed, wetting her dry mouth. She was probably carrying this too far, but she had to know, didn't she? 'I know the landowner's rights aren't completely decided in this issue, but, when it comes down to fact, what I do with my own property is my business. Who would know?'

'Get to the point, Alex.' There was an odd edge now to Jay's voice. His body seemed tense, waiting. 'Are you offering me the digging rights to this land?'

She kept her tone cool and businesslike, but her small face had whitened with strain. 'Are you interested? From what I've heard, it's still a fairly common practice.'

'But illegal... at least where graves are involved.' Long moments of silence, then Jay added so impassively that she could not have said which way he swayed, 'Do you have any idea how hard your father fought against this?'

Hope flared. Please, Jay, she thought, say no. Don't do this. Aloud, she pressed haughtily, 'Are you declining?'

His mouth twisted. 'To let the offer go elsewhere? No, I'm not declining.' He pushed both hands into jeans pockets. 'If you're serious I'll lease everything you have.'

Shock washed over Alex, sluicing pretence from her face, revealing disappointment and betrayal that she no longer wished to hide. 'No,' she said shakily, 'you won't. Because I retract. This site is not for sale... not at any price.'

'What do you mean, you retract?' Jay took a step towards her, looking positively dangerous. 'What's going on, Alex?'

'Work it out for yourself,' she cut in. 'I have to get back.' She pushed past him and because she couldn't get away quickly enough ran down the slope, blonde hair flying, heart bound by an icy web. Her brain, given free rein over self-recriminations, spoke up with a vengeance, calling her an idiot... a trusting fool. Men like Jay—or at least the Jay she had perceived him to be—truly *didn't* exist any more. His romantic pursuit had only been the means to an end. He was a fake.

She was aware of him following, heard him curse as she hurtled downhill. 'Don't be stupid, Alex! You'll break an ankle.'

'It's *my* ankle!' she retorted hotly. A sudden, sliding rustle told her that he'd barely escaped falling. Dry leaves shifted beneath her own boots, making the speed she'd adopted almost impossible. But she wouldn't give it up. She was running from an emotional assailant. A manipulator. The list went on... but then, anger was better than tears, especially when she sensed Jay gaining on her, breathing a little heavily but definitely there.

Afterwards she was never quite sure how it happened. She would have liked to credit Jay with a flying tackle, but, knowing he had more finesse than to bring down his prey in so brutish a manner, she eventually blamed a gnarled root for the fall. There was one heart-stopping moment of capture before she tripped and took Jay with her, his body instinctively shielding her as they tumbled down the hill.

As a result, he landed on top, his face so terrible a mixture of anger and concern that Alex barely looked up before closing her eyes tightly again. 'Are you hurt?' he demanded. When she managed to shake her head he gritted from between clenched teeth, 'Then let me make a suggestion: you want my attention in the future, you find a sane way of getting it.'

Alex's eyes flew open again, glittering with unspoken accusations. 'Let me up.'

Jay raised his upper body a few inches, but from the waist down he remained a heavy and disturbing weight. 'As soon as you tell me just what you were trying to prove.'

'*Disprove,*' she corrected tersely. 'And I'm referring to my suspicions.'

'Which were?'

'Which *are,*' Alex tried and failed to stare him down, 'that you have absolutely no loyalty for my father, and very little respect for the dead. A couple of glaring faults... even for the nicest man alive.'

'Alex, come on! Of all the ridiculous——'

'Exactly!' she cut him off. 'To think I actually trusted some strange guy who wanted to clean my flue, and cook my breakfast, and introduce me to his family, and,' she accused wildly, 'rock me to sleep. It is pretty ridiculous.' For all the emotion in her voice, her face seemed set in stone. 'Now get off me, Jay.'

If she had expected some obvious reaction she was disappointed. Jay held her eyes, neither attempting to placate her nor obeying her dictate to move. He seemed hard and contained still, as if she was the one at fault. 'Let's hear the rest of it.'

'You *know* the rest of it.' She struggled, limbs shaking with agitation. 'You let me think you were genuine...the greatest guy to come along since Cary Grant. But all the time you were just using me.'

'How?' He subdued her efforts again; she felt like a frustrated child.

'To get past Ty. You brought me up here because you wanted permission to dig. Then, when you found me in sympathy with my father's view, you carried it one step further. ''Youth Risks All to Claim His Destiny'',' she reeled off in a bitter voice. 'Touching story, Jay, but I couldn't buy it. And my instincts were good, for once. You agreed to that lease.'

'You seemed serious.' His tone was glacial. 'If I'd said no, what was to keep you from approaching some other prospect... some guy who cared zilch about ancient history and culture, but plenty about the dollar? There's a tremendous commercial demand for relics, Alex. I've seen sites that were literally strip-mined for grave goods... a practice that I personally find immoral.'

'That's right.' Alex had seen one of those places, too. 'You only have a *scientific* interest in relics. That's why your cabin is decorated in early aborigine,' she taunted recklessly. 'Sort of a mini-museum.'

'Cut it out, Alex.'

'A little too close to home? I won't apologise.' She strained against him, eyes filling afresh. 'Yesterday when I asked where those artefacts came from, and you said "here and there", I just assumed you'd bought them at some exhibition or another. Collectors tend to be touchy about their sources, right? Then you brought me up here and you started talking about archaeology and I started to catch on, only now you don't believe in digging, and frankly I don't know what to believe.'

'You should have let me finish the story.'

'I heard enough.' Alex went limp as her muscles gave way. 'I heard the part where my father ordered you off his land. How could you let me believe you were close to him? How could you tramp around as if you owned the place?'

'Because I was,' Jay said flatly. 'And I do.'

'Wh... what?'

Eyes smouldering, Jay took advantage of her confusion to press home the truth. 'We crossed my boundary line, Alex. This is part of the land Ty sold me six years ago, before I built the cabin.'

'He wouldn't do that!' Bewilderment slowly overtook her suspicion. 'Why would he do that? Knowing how you felt?'

'Because I feel differently now.' Jay made an impatient sound. 'Look, I don't even surface hunt any more. I haven't added a piece to my collection since I was twenty-four years old, but yes, I display it. I may not be proud of how I got some of those relics, but I am proud of my heritage.

'Ty was partly responsible for changing my mind...about a lot of things. When he sold me this land he was, in effect, passing down guardianship of the fort——' He broke off, steely-eyed. 'But I won't bore you with the touching details.'

He rolled off her, and, for all the energy Alex had expended trying to free herself, she felt cold without him. She sat up, as he did, and pushed a shaking hand through her hair. 'If you already own the fort, why did you say you'd lease it?'

'I said I'd lease everything you had. There are sites on your part of the homestead, too, Alex. A rock cave in the cliff, a couple of mounds...enough to attract interest, unscrupulous or otherwise.'

'I don't know what to say.' She felt stupid and completely miserable. 'I just...everything seemed to fall into place up there. I thought you were playing me along...to get something you wanted.'

'The way you thought I was playing you off Jake and Paula last night?'

'I'm really sorry.'

'Oh, yeah?' Jay narrowed his eyes, then began to brush bits of debris off his shirt. 'Well, I haven't decided whether to kiss you or cut a switch off a tree. You tried to protect something you believe in. And you stood up for Ty...I admire that. But you also made some insulting accusations. We have a saying around here: a man is nothing without his good name.'

'I'm sorry,' Alex said again, in a small voice. 'You have a very good name with me.'

'I should. I've worked hard enough to earn it.' He rounded on her, any grudging allowance for humour gone. 'I've never met a more cynical, wary, *paranoid* young woman. You don't have a lot of faith in people, do you, Alexandra?'

She flinched, but admitted, 'No. No, I don't.'

'Why?'

Alex stared at him, wondering whether he'd ever really *seen* the outside world...compared it to his own? Did he think everyone lived this way? Happily in one another's pockets, sharing everything, belonging? A sudden bitterness flooded through her. She turned away, eyes scanning the middle distance, voice taut. 'Not everyone comes from a family like yours, you know. All safe and warm and *nurturing*.'

'Am I supposed to apologise for that? What kind of family do you come from?'

Alex savagely brushed pine needles from her up-drawn knees. 'The kind that cares more about public image than personal relationships. The kind where you're expected to take your place and do you job and try to be a credit to the rest of them, even though your efforts never measure up.' She scooped up some acorns, ground them together in her fist. 'The kind you can count on to tear down your successes and magnify your failures.'

Her voice shut off abruptly, and Jay said nothing. She let the acorns drop and dusted her palms. Already she regretted talking so much...exposing so many raw nerves. She wouldn't blame him if he branded her a neurotic and took to the hills. 'I'm sorry,' she said flatly. 'You don't need this.'

'Don't tell me what I need.' His tone was husky, impatient. 'I'm sorry, too, Alex. I'm sorry you weren't raised in a happy, secure environment. I'm sorry you can't trust people. I'm sorry you're so damned suspicious of every gesture I make.' He caught her shoulders and brought her around to face him. 'I'm not the enemy.'

No, he wasn't the enemy. If she could only work out who or what *was* then she might settle this gnawing anxiety. She might throw away the sleeping pills, and forget the nightmares, and feel like a whole person again. 'I know.' She met his eyes for a long moment before tears welled. 'You've been very good to me.'

'Still searching for obscure motives?' he demanded a bit roughly.

'No...just feeling thankful.'

Jay stared down, not with the smile she halfway expected, but with his eyes dark and mouth grave. 'Then I'm going to be honest with you,' he said. 'I do want something. I want first option on your property if you sell. I'm telling you now, up front, because I won't risk causing doubts later. Any problem with that?'

Alex swallowed, considering, then shook her head.

'Good.' Jay nodded. 'I've said it; now you can forget it until the time comes. Just know that my wanting Ty's land had nothing to do with my personal feelings for you.'

Alex rubbed the back of one hand across her damp eyes, wanting almost desperately to lighten his mood. 'That sounds encouraging. Could it be you have a strange weakness for irrational, hysterical——?'

'Pink-nosed blondes?' Jay finished drily. 'As a matter of fact, I do. And if your tummy rumbles again I'll be a complete push-over.' He got to his feet, involuntarily wincing as he dusted off his clothes. 'Come on, sweetheart.' He stretched down a hand. 'You need something to eat, and I need a hot shower. Then, if I can forget you rolled me over a mountainside, we'll talk.'

CHAPTER SIX

ALEX had never been so unsure of her appearance. Yet she loved the clothes she wore. The outfit was like a fantasy, it was so far removed from her normal style. She felt a bit like a rock star in it, and frankly a little silly, but no way would she risk hurting Christina's feelings by backing out now.

She leaned close to the mirror to apply mascara, eyes darkening as she sensed another attack of nerves coming on. This wasn't her first date, for heaven's sake! It wasn't the prom, or one of Robert's business dinners, or dancing till midnight with a relative stranger. She had no corsage pins or stuffy conversations to dread. No need to wonder what filet mignon and a carafe of red wine might be worth in terms of her escort's behaviour. Jay was, after all, no stranger.

Alex had been with him almost constantly during the past five days, touring his mother's farm from top to bottom, from the hay-filled timbers of the great barn to the low-lying stretch of river bottom with its dense canebrake. She'd had her first ride on a John Deere tractor, standing up beside him as he drove back and forth, turning winter-hard earth to the air. She'd had her first ride horseback, too... not on Brady, who was barely broken and too spirited for a beginner, but high atop a gentle mare named Nell.

And, on the days when they hadn't been at Laura's, they had roamed the woods. Jay had shown her an effigy mound—a bear-shaped heap of earth and stone where ancient Indians once conducted worship, his descriptions of their ceremonies and rituals so vivid that the fine hair had stood up on Alex's nape. By the time they had explored an old campsite near the mouth of the creek Alex had been strangely intrigued by the past, and deeply drawn to her guide.

So why nervous?

She twirled colour on to her bottom lashes and intently met her eyes in the glass. Because this was the first time he had actually asked her out? No, that wasn't true either. The invitation had been more a dare than anything else. She'd asked what teenagers found to do in such a quiet little town, and Jay had answered with an enigmatic smile, 'Enough.'

So Alex had impulsively challenged him to show her. That had been yesterday. And this morning, just as impulsively, she had found herself buying paint at Joe's Hardware and asking Jay's sister-in-law what to wear on a Conway County Saturday-night date.

'Something sexy,' Christina had advised. There had been a moment's speculation. Then, hazel eyes dancing, she had pulled Alex down the tool aisle, through a stockroom, and into living quarters behind the shop. The apartment was small, but pretty, its mauve and blue colour scheme set off by country pine furniture and lots of lace.

'I get all my paint and wallpaper at cost,' Christina had shrugged off Alex's compliment, 'and decorating makes a nice substitute for my old hobby. *Clothes*,' she elaborated with a wry downward grin. 'When I started having babies I had to give them up for sacks. But I kept them around for sentimental reasons.' She started rummaging through a bedroom cupboard, 'In here, I think. What size are you?'

'Three, but you don't have to——'

'This is a five...close enough. Do you have some jeans that fit kind of tight?'

'Well, yes, but——'

'Great. Try this on.' Christina tossed her a soft garment that seemed to be made of leather. 'The boots, too,' she instructed, turning away to riffle the contents of a small cedar box. 'And jewellery. You need jewellery.'

The tunic was doeskin, Alex had since decided, dyed to palest grey and fashioned in a soft jacket-like shape that fell just past her hips. The shoulders were lightly padded, and across the breast, the back, and the cuffs swung a seductive leather fringe. That same fringe decorated the matching half-boots. Into them Alex had tucked her skinniest, sexiest jeans. 'You look like a call-girl,' she told her reflection. But her eyes stared back, exquisitely made-up and excited, Christina's turquoise pendant nestled a little closer between her breasts, and she vowed to enjoy the transformation.

The look in Jay's eyes made instant impact. 'Wow!' he muttered, voice low and hoarse, head snapping back a little as if hit by an unexpected jolt. Alex felt it herself... a steady pulse of electricity that caught her up and made her bold.

'Wow, yourself.' She openly looked him up and down, liking the denim jeans and jacket, the black body-moulding T-shirt. 'Do you want to come in?'

'Don't tempt me,' he warned drily. 'Not if you want to get through this date.'

Alex gave a small smile and turned, aware of Jay's eyes on her backside while she gathered up her handbag and locked the front door. 'That does it. Where to?'

'Nowhere specific.' He handed her into the Blazer, his tone unnatural now, practically forced. 'Just cruising. You have heard of cruising, haven't you, city girl?'

'Of course.'

By the time they had made one pass around the main streets of McGee, Alex knew something had gone terribly wrong. Jay had barely spoken since he had backed out of her driveway, and when he did speak it was without eye-contact. His glances hit her forehead, or her temple, and then moved back to the road. He was there, sitting beside her, yet she couldn't shake the impression that he was *avoiding* her.

'You know, Jay,' she began uncertainly, 'you should have said so if you didn't want to be pushed into this date.'

'It isn't that.' He seemed dark and brooding and faintly harassed. 'I wanted to be with you tonight.'

'Then what's the problem? Why won't you look at me?'

'I've seen you.'

'Oh.' Alex stared at his profile, at the leaping muscle in his jaw. Her heart sank like a leaking balloon. 'You don't like the outfit.'

'I love the outfit,' he gritted softly. 'I was *bowled over* by the outfit. I just don't understand it, Alex.' The muscle leapt with a little more vigour. 'Do you have any idea how much restraint the last week has cost me? I spent an entire night with you in my bed, in my arms, and didn't make a move! And now this...' Finally he looked at her, his face shadowed with frustration. 'Why are you doing this?'

Alex's blue-grey eyes widened, darkened. 'You think I'm trying to *seduce* you?'

'Aren't you?'

'*No.* Well... a little,' she stumbled, flushing, 'but not completely.' Then today's anxiety began to make sense. She started to get angry and her voice rose a decibel. 'What's wrong with wanting to be seductive anyway? Maybe I'd like a sign. Some proof that I haven't been demoted to little sister. Have you thought about that?'

His mouth crooked grudgingly. 'You aren't little-sister material.'

'Then who am I?'

'When you opened the door tonight, and I saw you standing there...' He paused as if to find concise words. 'Well, I thought you were a vision out of my dreams. All this holding back caught up with me and turned into something different. Good old-fashioned lust.' His eyes narrowed. 'Does that shock you, sweetheart? You asked for it.'

'I asked for an explanation.'

'Right,' he agreed impassively. 'You're Ty's daughter.'

'That's ridiculous!'

'Why? I had a lot of respect for the man. It didn't sit well to find myself lusting after his daughter.'

'Well, I'm glad to see you're over it,' she said on a scathing note. 'I'm glad to see that the great gentleman's code is once again in operation.' She turned to stare out of the window, baffled and yet curiously honoured. 'Oh, brother!' she muttered under her breath. Then impulsively she turned back around. 'Tell me something, Jay. Are you good at pretending?' She took his cocked brow for assent. 'Then pretend I'm just me...Alexandra. Pretend there are no complications. Pretend we met legitimately at... oh, a barn dance or something...'

He reached out to flick a bit of fringe. 'Should I pretend you're wearing a gunny sack?'

'Whatever gets you through the night.' She slanted a complicated look his way. 'And I won't ask you to do anything that makes you uncomfortable.'

Jay threw back his head to laugh, his attitude suddenly younger, carefree. 'OK,' he gave in drily, 'I'm all for recreating simpler times. Come over here!'

'Where?' Alex began to slide along the seat towards him. 'Here?'

'No...closer.'

'Jay, if I move any closer I'll be straddling the gear stick!'

'Exactly,' he said with satisfaction. 'Now, watch me. This is reverse, neutral, first, second, third, and fourth. Got it?'

'Got it? What do you mean, got it?' She stared at him, frantic. 'We're going to have an accident!'

'Not if you do your part. I'll work the clutch, and when I say "shift", you shift. See... now I have a free arm to put around you.' He unhurriedly suited the action to words. 'Understand?'

'Well, yes, but...' her voice lost substance as she adjusted to having Jay close, very close '...help me if I get lost, will you?'

She did get confused a couple of times, but although Jay winced at the grating gears he didn't yell or glower. His big hand covered her small one to guide her through the moves, then dropped to her thigh afterwards, making Alex wonder whether it was one of those planned manoeuvres that men did... like yawning and stretching at the movies. She couldn't help enjoying it, though, and sat all a-quiver while he lightly kneaded her flesh, eyes on the road as if it weren't happening.

'I'm starved.' He pointed out a small restaurant. 'Let's stop there.'

Alex changed gear and together they brought the Blazer to a crawl. The car park was filled to overflowing, yet Jay managed to find a slice of parking space that left only a portion of his rear bumper in the road. Alex peered cautiously into the traffic, hand on the doorknob while she watched for the best moment to hop down.

'Whoa! Don't get out, sweetheart.' Jay grasped her shoulder, laughing. 'We're dining at the only place in town that still offers kerb service.'

Alex gazed around: all the vehicles were indeed occupied. 'My mistake,' she said uncomfortably, her eye on the teenage waitress who was striding towards them. 'Do I at least get a menu?'

'Sure.' Jay pointed out a well-lit signboard bolted to the side of the building. 'But I can order for both of us, if you like.' Alex nodded, and he in turn smiled at the girl who had appeared in his window. 'How are you doing, Mary Beth? We'll have two double cheeseburgers...no onion, two large fries with ketchup, two cherry Cokes, and——' he paused while she wrote '—a pack of Juicy Fruit gum.'

'Got it, Mr McGee.' The redhead lifted pretty blue eyes from her note-pad. 'Or should I call you Jay? I mean, I'm not one of your students any more.'

'You'll always be one of my students, Mary Beth.' The warmth in Jay's voice took the edge off his refusal. 'I'm too proud of you to see it any other way.'

The girl flushed and scribbled busily on the pad for a moment. Then, edging a quick glance towards Alex, she imparted, 'I'm attending Eastern now. As and Bs.'

'No kidding! Have you decided on a major?'

'Interior design.'

'Ahh. So you'll be leaving home for the big city one day?'

'You'd better believe it. I'd leave tonight if it weren't for my kids.' Then a horn honked for service and she swiftly tapped a hand against Jay's truck door. 'Gotta go. I'll have your food in a few minutes.'

'Did she say kids?' Alex breathed when the waitress had moved on.

'Twin boys,' Jay confirmed. 'They'd be about two now. Mary Beth isn't married,' he added without judgement. 'When I met her last year she was sixty pounds overweight, dangerously low on self-esteem, and without prospects...not even this part-time job. My mother had worked like the devil to snatch her back from Drop-Out Land. Now the boys are in a special day-care and she's getting an education. One day she'll be off welfare completely.'

'Nice story,' Alex said softly, sincerely. 'Where do you fit in?'

'A history course last summer. Some tutoring towards a GED.' He shrugged. 'My mother is the real driving force. She makes these kids think. She wants them to be somebody, and she makes them want it too.'

'Do a lot of teenagers end up leaving McGee?'

'Oh, yeah.' Jay admitted. 'I did it myself. McGee may be home, but beyond that it's like any other small town... few jobs, little cash flow, slow change. It's a scary feeling to come of age and see your life stretching ahead of you without opportunity.'

'My grandfather used to say that the cure of every small town is industry.'

'And the leaders of this community expend a lot of effort trying to attract it,' Jay assured her. 'But every time we get a company interested they want better roads, or larger power capacities, or special waste facilities. All those things take money, Alex. We don't have money. That's the point.'

'Then use something you do have,' she challenged after a moment of chewing her lip. 'Use your natural resources. This county backs up to the Daniel Boone National Forest... why not steal some of the thunder? Go for the tourists. Better yet, go for something more permanent. There must be a lot of people out there... people exactly like me... who would sell their souls for a little cabin in the woods. Some place where they could vacation, or retire, or just get away from the——'

'I like seeing you all fired up,' Jay interrupted in a mild voice, and she knew that he wasn't taking her seriously. 'When you go back to Louisville you can tell the world what a wonderful place Conway County is.

Maybe even line up a group of time-share investors. But for right now,' he gave her hand a conciliatory squeeze, 'let's eat. OK?'

Alex's appetite shrivelled along with her enthusiasm. She hated having her ideas brushed aside. No matter how friendly the disguise, such tactics smacked of Robert, and left her feeling deflated. But then, wasn't it time she stopped seeking approval for every thought that entered her head? Jay didn't realise that she could easily do what he'd suggested. Tell the world—or at least a few hundred thousand magazine readers—about Conway County. Create a verbal portrait to spark interest from any direction.

Feeling better, she bit into one of the cheeseburgers Mary Beth had brought, finding it topped with coleslaw and surprisingly good. 'My mother disapproved of fast food,' she told Jay between bites. 'Most kids go to McDonald's regularly, but for me it was a rare and very special treat.'

'Poor, deprived Alex.' He popped a French fry into her mouth. 'You can consume anything you want when you're with me.'

'But think of the cholesterol. The sodium. The fat.'

'I'm trying not to,' he chided. 'I don't eat this way often, but when I do I enjoy every bite.' With boyish charm and a total disregard for his health, he eyed Alex's abandoned food. 'Aren't you going to finish that?' She shook her head, smiling, and in five minutes flat he had polished off her burger and the last of the fries. Then he unwrapped a stick of gum for each of them.

'Where to now?' she wondered when he had disposed of their rubbish and started the engine.

'To Jake's.' Jay grinned. 'Cruising takes fuel.'

They drove down the street in style, music pulsing from the speakers, windows half open, hair blowing. Alex noticed teenagers gathered at nearly every car park, sipping Cokes beneath overhead lights, or paired off in their cars, talking. Occasionally one of them recognised Jay's Blazer and waved, and he lifted his hand to return the greeting. Each time his arm settled back across her shoulders Alex shifted closer, her heart thudding with suppressed excitement. The first stars of night twinkled high above. The truck was impossibly intimate, the air between them heavy with tension.

She couldn't hide her relief at finding someone other than Jake manning the fuel pumps. Jay laughed at her transparent expression and gestured towards the white Trans Am parked on a side-yard. Light glowed from Jake's apartment over the garage—just a couple of candles, from the looks of it. 'Unless I miss my guess,' Jay drawled near her ear, 'my brother is being treated to one of Paula's gourmet meals... among other things.'

'Such as a lesson on table manners?' Alex came back drily. She was secretly elated by Jay's amusement. If he'd wanted Paula for himself then finding her upstairs with Jake would hardly please him.

'You might be surprised,' he deflected the insult. When they were back on the road, though, he added seriously, 'There's a lot more to Jake than you think, Alex. I hope you'll give him another chance.'

'For you,' she quipped softly, 'anything. Jake and I might even become friends.' Secretly calculating the improbability of *that*, but making a mental note to try harder, she peered into the velvety darkness. 'Where are we going?' She had expected Jay to head towards town again, and instead he'd turned the Blazer on to a narrow side-road which was totally unfamiliar.

'Just driving,' he said obliquely. 'There's nothing like a mountain road on a starry night.'

Alex couldn't suppress a giggle. 'Is that line handed down from brother to brother in your family?'

Jay grinned. 'It happens to be the truth. Just look at that sky.'

'I'm looking.' Alex gazed through the front window. 'Big Dipper,' she chanted in a soft voice. 'Little Dipper. North Star.' Her heart was fluttering all over the place. 'Where is this leading me, Jay?'

'Nowhere you don't want to go, I hope.'

He pulled the truck into a shadowy spot and switched off the engine, and Alex's heart slammed like a fist straight into her throat. For a moment she was sixteen again, gawky and uncertain. Then Jay reached for her, the lazy warmth in his eyes dissolving her fears. 'Come here,' he said huskily, cupping her head between his hands. 'Let me look at you.'

He did nothing else for a long moment, his gaze intense, hypnotic. Then his fingers slid into the silk of her hair and with a gentle tug he brought her head close.

He took his time over that first kiss, slowly brushing his mouth across hers, tasting the fullness of her lower lip, nipping at her tender flesh and then soothing the pleasurable pain with his tongue, until Alex felt starved for real contact. Eyes dark with frustrated desire, she tried to capture Jay's mouth. But his light caresses continued to tease her, driving her to the point where her fingers dug into his forearms and she whispered grittily, 'Stop.'

Laughing low in his throat, Jay pulled her up close. 'I don't think you mean that.'

Her flesh gave a long shudder in response to his; she wasted no effort on denial. Jay at last took her mouth, his quiet savagery blasting like a hot wind across the flame he'd kindled, and then she understood why he'd waited. Such a delicious sense of urgency! Her hands passed over his chest, marvelling at his feverish heat through the thin T-shirt, craving a more intimate touch. Woman power filled her, only for a moment, but long enough to pull the shirt free of his waistband, long enough to feel his heart pounding under her naked palm. Then she began to tremble—really tremble. Jay shifted closer, and the imprint of his body melted her bones.

Breath fogged the windows, creating a steamy, urgent world.

'I'd forgotten that making out could be like this,' Jay muttered hoarsely. 'On second thoughts, making out was *never* like this. Come here, sweetheart.' Half tortured, he eased her down into the seat, sliding over her with a contact and pressure and weight that she found unbearably erotic. His lean hand shook a little as he pushed it beneath the cool scented leather of her tunic and found no bra, just small rounded curves.

Alex arched against him, her hands in the warm, rich waves of his hair. 'Touch me.'

'I am touching you.' He groaned again, deep in his throat, so that she felt the vibrations. 'And you're touching me too, make no mistake about that. You're touching me in places I didn't know I had.' With trembling fingers he undid buttons, stroked silken flesh. He tasted her erratic pulse and the small spot where Christina's turquoise pendant had lain, and finally her breasts. Then his ragged sigh shuddered hot across her skin. 'In high school we called this getting to second base.' He drew back, a marked severity in his face. 'Time to stop.'

'I'll bet that tone of voice used to really scare your dates.'

'It isn't meant to scare you.' His laugh was strained, rasping. 'Sober you, maybe. Or me. My control is stretching pretty thin.'

'I'll take my chances with your control.'

'No, you won't. My parents raised me to be a——'

'Gentleman. Right. Don't I know it?' Resenting his self-imposed bounds, Alex fought desperately to bring her quivering body under rein. Then she realised that Jay was shaking, too. She lay still while he buttoned her clothes again, deciding in that moment, with his fingers so gentle against her skin, that she adored him exactly the way he was. 'Sir Galahad,' she whispered, her small hand pressed to his cheek. 'I take it second base is the limit?'

'For good books,' he agreed. And it didn't matter that he'd mixed his metaphors—she understood completely.

CHAPTER SEVEN

ALEX drove out to the McGee farm one evening the next week.

Laura seemed pleased to see her. She was alone—a rarity—and for twenty minutes or so they sat sipping coffee and chatting... about life on a farm, raising a large family, and Laura's involvement with the school system. Then she slid her empty cup on to the table and settled back. 'I know you aren't here to talk about me, Alex.' A faint smile accompanied the question, 'Which is it... Ty or Jay?'

Alex flushed guiltily. In personal situations she often took the place of interviewer. It was easier to listen than to speak; but then, she hadn't counted on Laura's intuition being as highly developed as her son's. 'My father,' she said precipitately. 'John Shawn told me about his carvings, and I was wondering... could I see them?'

'Of course.' Laura briefly patted her hand. 'Come with me.'

Alex followed her down the short hallway to a blue and ivory bedroom that she adored on sight. Neat, attractive, but completely unpretentious, it was like the rest of this lovely old farmhouse... a reflection of Laura McGee's personal style.

'Ty sold most of his work to speciality shops,' her hostess explained while opening a tall curio cabinet, 'and some of it he made for friends, but everything was one of a kind.' From the top shelf she handed down a tiny humming-bird, exquisitely poised on a carved branch.

'My favourite,' she said softly. 'Pieces like this can't be mass-produced.'

Alex drew her fingertips across the impossibly fragile beak. Ty had been a gifted craftsman, no doubt about that! But, while the extreme sensitivity of his work impressed her, she couldn't help wondering why he'd kept at it. There was obviously little pay involved. The hours must have been long and very lonely, whereas a regular job would have given him a chance to meet new people... perhaps even re-marry.

Alex replaced the humming-bird as another carving from the group drew her eye. The Indian maiden was perhaps ten inches high, fine-boned, barefooted and quite beautiful, a water pot in her arms. 'May I?' she murmured, lifting the small statue down. She stared into the lovely proud face with its doe eyes and full mouth, and her heart inexplicably began to beat faster. Her skin tingled as she fingered the smooth garments, and for a moment she was back at the ancient fort, Jay's arms around her as they envisaged the long-dead village to which a young woman like this one might have belonged.

'A lot of Ty's work involved Indian figures,' Laura was saying. 'He had a great love and respect for my grandmother's race... this was his way of showing it.' Pausing, she asked, 'Are you all right?'

'Yes.' Alex traced the figure's long braid over a proud, slim shoulder, passing off the strange sensation as melancholia. Her father had devoted so much time to these little lumps of wood. What thoughts had accompanied all that solitude? Had he ever thought of her?

She glanced up to find Laura still watching her, black eyes intent. 'Maybe we should talk about Alex,' she suggested quietly. 'You seem upset.'

'Yes.' Alex let out a slow breath. 'I am a little.' Yet she was not quite sure where to start. 'A couple of days ago,' she began haltingly, 'I took Ty's clothes out of the armoire and packed them up. I found some things in a drawer. His carving tools. The truck keys. And a snapshot of them together. My mother was smiling up at him as if she had the whole world by the arm. And he...my father,' she said softly, 'well, he was very handsome and clean-cut, and he looked...I don't know, shy and solemn, but intense, too, as if he would protect her from anything.' She paused to lick dry lips. 'That picture showed me how they once felt about one another. I'd like to understand what happened.'

Laura paused, inwardly struggling to soften the truth. 'They were in love, Alex. Young and impulsive. They married one afternoon, arriving in McGee that same evening, and by the next sunrise Ty was out in the fields. That was your mother's orientation to being a farmer's wife. She barely saw her husband. She felt like an unwelcome guest in her mother-in-law's home. So she started spending time here. She used to call herself my apprentice.' A faint smile touched her mouth, reminding Alex for a moment of Jay. 'Our days were an endless round of dirty dishes, dirty laundry, ironing, mending, and hungry boys, but Elise always came back. She was homesick and, by that time, pregnant. I suppose we helped fill the void.'

Alex felt a pang of empathy as she tried to assimilate this changing picture of her mother. Newlywed, house help, exiled daughter. 'It sounds as if the marriage had started to fail before I was born.'

'There was a strain, yes, although things improved a little that spring. Ty fixed up his grandfather's cabin, the one where you're staying now, and they were finally able to live on their own. Elise tried to be content. You have to realise, though, that she was a beautiful girl, used to wearing pretty things, used to having pretty things around her. Ty did the best he could, but with money so tight...'

Laura trailed off, a trace of sadness behind her eyes. 'I'll never forget the night you were born. They arrived on my doorstep, soaked through with rain, dripping all over the place, laughing like a couple of nervous kids, and I remember thinking, Everything will be all right now. This baby will bring them together. Within fifteen minutes we had a fully fledged thunderstorm, and Elise had gone into hard labour. There was no question of driving eighty miles to a hospital in that downpour. Jason went after the local doctor and we settled in to wait.'

Laura paused at length. Alex saw grief surge into her black eyes and then gradually subside. 'One of my sons died in Vietnam, Alex. Did Jay tell you? He was Jesse...Jacob's twin, and I had my first and only brush with what Elise experienced when the two of them were born. I didn't want anything to do with them, you see. I didn't hold them. I wouldn't feed them. Jason had to buy formula and bottles. I didn't care. It lasted four days, until one of them—Jacob, I think—screamed with colic in the middle of the night. Without even thinking, I picked him up and held him to my breast. He stopped crying, I started crying, Jason held us both, and that was the end of it.' She clasped her hands together as if the memory still pained her. 'With Elise there was no end.'

'You're talking about post-natal depression.'

'Yes. The worst case I've ever seen.' Laura's eyes were still glittery with emotion. 'It was a short but very difficult labour, and afterwards Elise was non-responsive...too shocked and tired to even look at you. We thought she only needed some rest.'

'But rest didn't help?' Alex guessed thinly.

'No. The three of you stayed on here until Ty learned to take care of you. He did everything for you...changed your diapers, fed you, bathed you, dressed you. You became his baby, and in a sense so did Elise. He had to remind her to bathe, to change clothes, to eat. She was like a lost little girl.'

'Couldn't anyone help her?'

'The doctor gave her antidepressants and vitamins and told Ty to be patient.' Laura shook her dark head. 'In time she did get better, but she was never the same Elise. The Elise that I knew wouldn't hurt Ty the way she hurt him.'

Alex lay awake that night, brooding over the things Laura had told her and finally seeing the past take shape. A state of depression could make even everyday pressures seem insurmountable. Add to that some very real problems like culture shock, scraping for money, and the emotional withdrawal of her family, and one could easily understand her mother's desire to flee Conway County. But why break so ruthlessly from a man she had once loved?

For that matter, why deny Alex all contact with her natural father? By most accounts, Ty had been a man of deep sensitivity, a man whose presence would have enriched his daughter's life. Instead, Alex had known only Robert's ambivalence and suffered for it.

Subsequent thoughts of her writing haunted her, and she lay staring at the rough-beamed ceiling, remembering the other reason why she'd come to Conway County, and realising that she'd done absolutely nothing to sort out her career. But what did a woman do when her work left her cold? How, after months and months of apathy, did she go about recapturing the excitement? That 'I have something to say, aren't words miraculous?' feeling. Without it, she was less than whole.

She thought about Ty's Indian maiden, and wondered if that same urgency had driven him to create her. Was it coincidence that she resurrected the beauty and dignity of a forgotten people? Or had Ty brushed away the shavings, beheld her from a small distance, and sanctioned, 'Go speak for me, uphold my cause'?

Having witnessed the small statue's ability to do just that, Alex had to believe the latter. And if her father's creation could speak for him so eloquently then wasn't it possible for Alex to make a statement too? Tell the world in general, and Robert's memory in particular, that she was a serious writer with something to say?

She sat straight up in bed, a kind of cognition starting at the roots of her hair and trickling down her spine to the very tips of her toes as she thought about the story she'd once been incapable of writing, the story that had marked her an emotional, green kid in Robert's eyes. Not only did the subject still matter to her personally, but it was important to her father and to Jay. On a more practical note, it involved politics, academics, tradition, religion, human interest, and free enterprise. Serious food for thought. Botch it and it was a confusing mess, but handle it well and she might finally prove herself.

Alex knew that the magazine had printed nothing on the Indian artefacts controversy since state law had made the desecration of a burial site a felony. Nor had she seen any other media coverage. But the complicated issue had hardly been resolved. Wasn't it time for an update? If she presented her uncle with a *fait accompli*, and it was good, wouldn't he be compelled to use it? Couldn't it, by rights, cancel out that previous failure?

By Friday her research was in full swing. Alex sat propped against the headboard of her bed, piles of reference books surrounding her, a half-filled notebook balanced on her up-drawn knees. Wisps of hair escaped a hasty pony-tail. Her face was clean-scrubbed and intense, glowing in the light of a single burning lamp that had effectively disguised the evening shadows. The knock on her door caught her completely off guard.

Jay! She immediately shoved the books aside and swung her legs over, wincing at the cramp of muscles which had held one position too long. She had meant to stop working before now, to put on some make-up. She even considered darting into the bathroom for a hairbrush, but the second knock was too insistent, and she found that her own impatience far outweighed vanity.

She flung open the door, ready to rain kisses on him, ready to be greeted in a manner befitting their week-long separation, but one look from Jay killed the impulse. His eyes burned into her, dark with strain. His body, still clad in shirt and tie from the classroom, seemed stiff with tension and completely disinclined to embrace her.

Poised on the threshold, Alex stood shivering with shock, trying to read his face against the backdrop of starless night, finally murmuring without either of them having voiced a greeting, 'You'd better come inside.'

Jay followed her into the house, closing the door and leaning against it, his jaw tightening as he scanned the room with its hoard of books, books everywhere. His eyes came back to Alex, their expression bitter. 'Just tell me one thing,' he demanded tersely. 'Why did you lie about being a journalist?'

Alex swayed with marginal relief. Was that all? But then, judging from Jay's behaviour, it was perhaps a greater sin than she had believed. Emotions chased across her small face... surprise, guilt, self-deprecation. Why hadn't she been straightforward? She wet her mouth and managed to ask, 'How did you know?'

'Someone left last month's copy of *Kentucky!* in the staff lounge. I was curious after the things you'd told me, so I picked it up.' His gaze narrowed accusingly. 'You write as Alex Bannon.'

'Yes.' Her back went rigid and her hackles rose for an instant in the familiar way. 'But not to trade on my grandfather's reputation. Bannon is my second name.

It's legitimate, and appropriate. Grandfather encouraged me to write...to join the magazine staff. Robert never did.'

'So you do it to disassociate yourself from Robert?'

'More or less.' She shrugged uncertainly. 'Does it really matter why? I was going to tell you tonight.'

Jay ground out, 'Were you?'

'*Yes.*' His badgering was starting to get to her; frustrated, she held up a hand. 'Look, I was in tenth grade, writing for the school newspaper, when I changed my byline. Robert had brutally criticised a piece that I wrote on the student body elections. Dropping his name was my way of retaliating. A mute protest.' Her mouth quirked with remembered bitterness. 'I doubt he noticed.'

Jay seemed unmoved. 'Was it a good piece?'

Alex ran a hand through her pale hair, loosing part of it from the holder, distractedly freeing the rest. 'A few years ago I would have answered yes to that. Now I don't know.' She rolled the terry band over her wrist, her blue-grey eyes large and wary as she struggled to put pent-up feelings into words. 'I grew up believing that I belonged with the magazine, OK? That I had a God-given talent to write. I guess it was easy to believe in myself with Grandfather Bannon supporting me every step of the way, but when he died and Robert took over the editor's desk my confidence began to crumble. I started to believe him when he said I had no talent.' Her voice shook. 'I felt like a fraud.'

Emotion flickered in Jay's eyes, too fleeting to offer any real comfort. Stepping closer, he gritted, 'I felt like a fool when I opened that magazine.'

'Jay, I'm sorry. I never intended to mislead you. It just...happened that way. I was feeling down, and unsure of my identity, and...' She trailed off as he reached beyond her for one of the books.

For a moment he brushed so close that she felt his body heat, then he withdrew, mouth twisting when he'd read the book jacket. *'Ancient Indian Burial Methods.'* He lifted his head, his stance deceptively quiet. 'I'm obviously a gullible guy. Go ahead—give it your best shot.'

Her thoughts shifted, making room for new complications, seeing the broader picture now...not just his anger because she'd deceived him, but his suspicion connected to that deceit. Chin jutting, she insisted unhappily, 'I'm afraid the truth will have to do.'

'Assuming you're capable of it!'

Stung but determined to prove her innocence, Alex twisted round for her notebook and turned back to the first page. 'I'm writing a follow-up to the Indian relics question.' Holding out her notes, she urged, 'Take a look at this outline. I'm very excited about it! You see, for all the media attention the issue earned a couple of years ago, there's been very little said since...and I think people should know. Have the new laws made a difference, for instance? Are violators being prosecuted? And do most landowners now recognise the Indians' claim to the remains and possessions of his ancestors? In short, has anything changed?

'As Grandfather used to say, Stir a fire and keep it alive.'

But, if Alex had expected the truth to be her saving grace, Jay's black expression dampened any such hope. Ignoring the notes, he gritted, 'How is Conway County involved?'

'Only to the extent that there are dozens of campsites and burial grounds here, many of them undisturbed because people like you treat them with respect and honour. It's an important part of my piece...proving that human understanding and compassion sometimes prevail.'

Her claim made little impact; betrayal flared in his eyes. 'I was afraid you might do something like this! It's all I've been able to think about since I picked up that blasted magazine!'

'No, you've got it all wrong!' Alex shook her head and grasped his arm. 'I didn't *set out* to write this story. Until a few days ago the thought hadn't even crossed my mind. But I can get passionate about a subject in a hurry, particularly when it interests me. And you share the blame for the fact that this does interest me... very much. Yesterday I hiked up to the fort again. I stood there and ran a hand over those old stones, and I felt— I don't know,' she cast about for words, 'this shiver of awareness. As if there was something to be said. As if I had to say it.'

'Come on, Alex!' Jay impatiently shook her off. 'You saw an opportunity and you took it at my expense.'

'How can you suggest such a thing?'

'How can you deny it? I *confided* in you. I showed you places that I'd never show an outsider... sites your father asked me to protect. Does my trust mean that little to you?'

She fell back a step, hurt and shock in the look she flung him. 'It means everything!' Her heart constricted. 'That's why I didn't give specifics. I wouldn't do that to you... or him. The fort is safe, I swear.'

'It's not just the fort. Publish a piece like this and no site will be safe.' Jay's mouth curled. 'Why not just print an invitation while you're at it? "Welcome to Conway County, home of the untouched shrine." Better yet, give them a map.'

He was exaggerating...badly. Downtown, in McGee's own library, there was a wealth of information already in print. Alex had had no trouble finding it, and neither would anyone else who looked. For a moment she felt her blood heat with the impulse to lash out, but instead she sank on to the end of the bed, her face closing, the strain of many hours without rest or food suddenly bearing down hard. 'What do you want, Jay? Do you want me to give up the story?'

He thrust an impatient hand through his hair. 'I want you to be honest with me. More important—be honest with yourself. Was last week about you and me, Alex? Or were you just using me to impress your readers?' He looked disgusted, betrayed. 'Do you actually give a hoot in hell about anything else?'

Alex sucked in her breath, thinking that he could have kicked her in the stomach and offended her less. Anger washed over her like a sheet of flame, and this time she did not resist. 'It's my *job* to impress readers, Jay.' The words came from a hot, gravelly spot in the back of her throat. 'That's what I *do*. But I would never...' she haphazardly began ripping pages from her notebook '...*ever* delude someone I care about for the sake of a story. If you knew anything about me you'd know that. You'd also know——' she savagely aligned papers and tore '—that somewhere on my complicated list of reasons there was an idiotic desire to impress *you*!'

Something flickered in the back of his eyes. 'Alex, wait.'

'Why? Isn't this what you wanted?' Halved pages drifted to the floor. 'I'll return all these books to the library tomorrow. I'll call Kate and tell her I don't need that legal update after all. Relax, Jay. You win.'

Her small, polite voice hit its mark. A trace of colour skated over his cheekbones. 'I've hurt you.'

There was no answer to that. Alex got up and began to clear the mess. When the books were re-stacked in neat piles and the coverlet straightened she abruptly turned to face him again. 'You're the one who keeps pressuring me to make peace with myself,' she said bitterly. 'Until I overcome Robert's opinion of me it will never happen.' He stepped towards her then, and she flung up a staying hand. 'Don't. Nothing you do is going to help. In fact,' she crossed to the door and pointedly jerked it open, 'why don't we call it a night?'

She shivered as the darkness rushed in, and for a long moment their eyes clashed, her own more grey than blue, mutinous and resentful, and Jay's searching relentlessly. 'Just so long as you realise we aren't finished.' He abruptly ended the stand-off by stepping out on to the porch. 'I'll see you in the morning.'

She closed the door and leaned against it, feeling as if something cherished had died. After a while she gathered up the loose pages and shoved them into the wood-burning stove. Then she made coffee and sat down at the kitchen table, eyes bleak as she focused first on the milk pitcher she'd filled with jonquils, and then on the bed that dominated the small room.

The iron frame was freshly painted and the mattress spread with some white linens that Alex had found in the armoire. The hand-embroidery on the bed skirt and pillow cases looked like a simplistic version of her mother's needlework, the delicate pastel tones a perfect match for the quilt. Early in the week she had shopped for co-ordinating curtains, and snowy ruffled tiers now hung from new brass rods, making the log house seem airy and feminine.

But the changes which had so pleased her a few days ago now left her flat. If she had spent less time redecorating the cabin and more time thinking she might have seen the pitfalls of both her secrecy and her impulsive project. She might have tried to win Jay's support first, instead of crashing headlong and without warning into a territory so close to his heart.

But heavens, what an unreasonable man! Feeling wronged and misunderstood and completely miserable, Alex listened to the shallow tick of Ty's old clock. Eventually she got up and poured her cold coffee down the drain, then took her prescription bottle from a shelf and uncapped it. But, for the first time since her first night in this house, she did not shake one of the tiny pills into her hand.

From the kitchen window, through the trees, she could see Jay's light... still burning.

She opened the door to him early... with the last streaks of dawn still grazing the tree-tops and the air crisp with lingering frost. He stood tall and handsome on the porch, looking unbearably weary... and as strained as Alex felt. 'Will you come with me?' he asked huskily, without preamble. 'I think it's time you heard the rest of the story.'

After only a moment's hesitation Alex lifted her jacket from a hook and shrugged into it. She had been up and dressed for hours, the morning so chilly that she'd dragged a heavy sweater over her shirt and jeans. She was glad of her choice when she stepped outside and peered at the sky. 'It looks like rain,' she commented inconsequentially.

Jay's thick clothing and hooded poncho were proof that he'd drawn the same conclusion. 'There's shelter.'

Alex nodded. She hated being this way. Forced. Clipped. Wary. But, seeing no help for the situation, she kept silent and fell into step, matching his pace well beyond the tree line and up. Her breath hung before her like puffs of smoke, the air so brisk that inhaling hurt her lungs. The path grew steep, requiring more physical effort, and after a long stint of climbing she noticed that the trees had thinned, and that scattered rocks began to dot the ground.

The slope evened out momentarily, and Alex stood with hands on hips to catch her breath. It was almost straight up from here. The cliff was within sight, and she no longer had to guess at their destination. Jay was taking her to the rock house.

'You go first,' he instructed. 'Hold on to anything within reach, and move slowly.' Alex clung to scrubby bushes and vines to keep from sliding backwards, and once, with not even a rock to hold on to, she lost her footing and would have fallen, but Jay was there, his hand against her backside to give her a boost. 'We're almost there. You're doing fine.'

But her stressed muscles were quivering by the time they'd completed the ascent. Up at the top, she gripped Jay's arm tightly as they crossed a treacherously narrow ledge. A great rock overhang shadowed the other side, creating a cave which was perhaps twenty feet deep. Cold emanated from its stone floor and interior. It was dark but completely dry.

Jay left her standing near the opening. She heard the thud of wood hitting wood, and, as her eyes adjusted to the dimness, watched him arrange short branches and twigs. Presently the flame of a match illuminated his face. The twigs kindled and a lick of blue began to eat up the bark. 'I keep firewood stacked against the back wall,' he told her. 'The matches are in this tobacco can.'

Alex could not imagine wanting to visit the rock house alone, but she nodded. 'Thanks... I'll remember.' Shivering, arms crossed over her breasts, she moved closer to the growing fire. Halfway between herself and Jay she spied a deep round depression in the cave floor and with a small exclamation knelt down to examine it.

'The Indians valued a pockmark like that.' Jay quietly offered his knowledge. 'They would drop in a handful of grain and grind it with a stone pestle. Over time the depression was worn smooth inside, and because it was mainly used to pulverise corn it became known as a hominy hole.'

Alex nodded, her mind irresistibly conjuring up Ty's maiden in the flesh, sitting cross-legged on the hard floor, serenely grinding meal for bread while the golden light of a cooking fire flickered across stone walls. She watched Jay replace the matches in their niche. 'Do you come here often?'

'Whenever I have serious thinking to do.' His mouth twisted attractively. 'I got into the habit as a boy. You learn to appreciate solitude with six brothers around.'

'Solitude is overrated. Ask someone who got too much of it.'

'At least you had the luxury of making your mistakes in private.'

'No, actually I had them analysed to bits... but we aren't talking about me.' He was still on his haunches, tending the fire, and she eased down beside him. 'What mistakes, Jay?'

'Betraying my ancestors,' he said bluntly. 'Desecrating that warrior's grave. There were others, of course, but none seemed so important. I was too addicted to the thrill of discovery to let them bother me for long. It took my father's death to wake me up.'

'How do you mean?'

Firelight played over his face, defining the rigid muscle that leapt rhythmically along his jaw. 'You have to understand,' he said presently, 'that my decision to study archaeology constituted a family crisis. My grandmother publicly denounced me in the name of her people. My mother begged me to reconsider. At one time or another, I think, Ty and each of my brothers had a go at me. But I stood my ground.

'I stood my ground so well, in fact, that I earned my degree with honours. I'd only served a short apprenticeship before receiving a sizeable grant to excavate a site here in Conway County—a field we'd leased further up the mountain. I supervised every aspect of the project, hand-picked the undergraduate students, rented the camping equipment and tools, secured the permits... all of it. What a summer!' he reflected softly. 'But, no matter how proud I felt of my team and what we were accomplishing, it didn't alter the fact that my working here in the county only widened the rift between my family and me.

'I suppose that's what drew me to Gayle.' His lean face seemed all stark angles in the firelight, his hair and beard burnished. 'She was the only one of the undergrads who knew anything about my background,' he explained. 'We'd dated on and off during the past year, but neither of us had all that much free time. That summer, with the project constantly throwing us together, our attraction gained force.

'George—that's the farmer whose field we were leasing—had put most of the students up for room and board, but some of us had to camp. Being the director of the project, I chose to live on site, and somehow,' he paused a bit awkwardly, 'Gayle wound up sharing my tent.

'I fell in love with her,' he admitted darkly. 'Partly because of our shared work. Partly because she was sympathetic and understanding about my family at a time when I needed it in the worst way. But mostly because she was a vibrant, exciting girl who knew where she was going and how to get there.

'By the start of the next term we were talking marriage. Gayle and the other students had gone back to school and I'd stayed on to clean up a few details—cataloguing mostly—before I joined another project already in the works.' He picked up a stick and raked it through the coals. 'That's when Dad passed away.'

He paused so long after the bald statement that Alex's heart ached in sympathy. 'Gayle was deep into a term paper and begged off his funeral,' he continued, 'which was unquestionably the bleakest hour of my life. Afterwards I came up here to be alone. I'm not even sure what linked the two events together, but I somehow started thinking about that warrior I'd uncovered at seventeen. All those years he'd been only a scientific specimen, and then suddenly I began to see him for what he really was. A human being.

'Maybe it was guilt haunting me,' he suggested drily, 'but by the end of that night my imagination had given him a complete identity. He trapped rabbits and practised spear-throwing and grumbled when frogs got in the spring. He made love to his woman in sweet, tall grass. On a clear night he bundled his children in bearskins to show them the stars. He exulted when his corn grew.

'The point is, he had a *life*. He had a family who once wept over his grave, the way I wept over my father's. And their ceremony was no less sacred.

'The next day,' he imparted broodingly, 'I arranged to have an Indian ritual performed. According to my grandmother, it was the only way the disturbed warrior could continue his journey to the spirit world. Maybe it worked, because afterwards I felt at peace with myself.

'Gayle, of course, thought I was crazy—especially when I told her I was giving up archaeology. I needed a few more credits to earn a history degree. That meant going back to school. But we could still be married the following summer. I had it all worked out.' His mouth twisted over the recollection. 'Only it didn't work. Gayle was stunned, then furious. Seems she'd been counting on whatever clout I carried to secure her position in the programme. An enlightened history student was about as useful to her as a steam shovel, and considerably less desirable.

'Gayle graduated top of her class that spring. One of our professors recommended her to a position in Peru and she left without so much as a goodbye. I learned afterwards that she'd used our broken engagement as proof of her own dedication to the profession I'd betrayed. That, more than anything else, helped me get over her. But the whole thing left a bitter taste in my mouth.' He stared starkly into the flames. 'Driving home last night, I saw it all happening again. Same story, different girl.'

'Thanks.' Alex dashed a hand across her eyes. 'It's nice to know you have such a high opinion of me.'

'I once had a high opinion of Gayle,' he came back quietly. 'Honesty is everything to me. She knew that. Yet she let me believe she loved me, when all she really cared about was the prestige of working on my project and the possibility that I might advance her career.'

They sat silent for long moments, Alex struggling to assimilate what he'd told her, Jay struggling with dark thoughts. 'I guess what I'm trying to say is that, for several complex reasons, this issue is a part of me. It's personal. And, while I might feel an insane desire to have Alex the person know everything about me, Alex the journalist is another matter.' His eyes came level. 'Last night I could see only one reason why you'd kept your writing a secret...the obvious one.'

She searched his face. 'Journalists have a bad name that way.'

'You have a very good name with me.'

Alex knew when her own words were being used against her. She made the connection and swallowed, remembering the accusations she'd hurled at him that day at the fort...accusations which were both hurtful and unfounded. 'Point taken,' she said huskily. 'But I never meant to use you, Jay. I just wanted so badly to write something important.'

He sank down beside her on the rock floor, back against the wall, one knee drawn up. His eyes were intense in the light of the fire. 'Then do it. Write the story.'

Last night those words might have elated her. Now she only felt numb. 'Why the change of heart?'

'It's simple,' Jay said. 'I realised last night that I was out of line. I have no right to censor your subject matter, Alex. More to the point, I don't want this or any story coming between us.'

'I must have reached the same point,' Alex told him softly. 'I burned my notes.'

'Then start over,' he advised after a pause, 'if it's important to you. It's your choice, and who knows? Maybe you can open a few eyes. At any rate, I won't stand in your way.'

Alex felt tears gathering on her lashes. Outside the rain finally pelted down and she watched it fall past the mouth of the cave, knowing what Jay's offer had cost him, feeling that last bit of animosity slide away. But a kind of despair hovered on the fringe of her mind and she said huskily, 'Don't. I don't care about the story any more. I was only fooling myself. It would never see print.'

'You don't know that.'

'Don't I?' Alex bit her lip and turned back to him, her hair as pale as champagne in the firelight. Yearning lay like a dark shadow in her eyes. 'Would you just tell me something?' she urged thinly. She was amazed at the effort it took to ask. 'When you picked up that magazine... did you read any of my work?'

Had she imagined that flash of discomfort? A second later Jay's face was impassive. 'The O'Brien interview.'

Alex gave a tense nod. Dean O'Brien was barely eighteen years old, a brilliant jockey who had been slated to ride in the upcoming Kentucky Derby, but remained amazingly unaffected by the hoopla. He was an interviewer's dream... full of funny little insights into the racing world and its celebrities, yet very much the outsider looking in until it came to riding... a pleasure he described in fresh, moving, articulate prose. The piece had been very important to Alex. In truth, it still was. She tried to sound casual. 'So what did you think?'

'Alex...'

'Please. An honest opinion would mean a lot to me.'

He held her eyes across an over-long pause. 'I didn't care for the interview,' he admitted finally. 'Not that I saw anything wrong with the basic structure or the content. It read well. It was well-written,' he stressed. 'But it was also a pretty dry account of an exceptional young man. Dean O'Brien is in my freshman history class, Alex. I know him. And, frankly, my problem isn't with what you wrote about him, it's with what you *didn't* write.'

He paused again and she invited without expression, 'Go on. I asked for honesty, didn't I?'

'OK...' Jay grimaced faintly '...you told your readers that riding is only a sideline for Dean. He plans to be a veterinarian. But you didn't tell them that veterinary medicine has been an O'Brien tradition for countless generations.

'Dean graduated a year ahead of his high-school class. Fine,' he said evenly, 'that's an accomplishment. But what about the fact that he did it with a high-A average while working as an exercise boy to earn spending money?

'Dean is a gifted rider. I agree. But did you mention that his size barred him from even the second-string football team when he wanted to be a quarterback so bad that he could taste it?' He stopped talking to watch her for a moment. 'Do you understand what I'm saying?'

'That Dean O'Brien is a genuine person, not a fact sheet?' Alex ventured, voice soft. Her mouth twisted into a reminiscent little smile. 'An Irishman who takes bagpipe lessons? I thought that was priceless.'

'Then why didn't you use it?'

'I wanted to.' Alex edged closer. 'I wanted to say that he reminded me of a tiger kitten...sleek and quick and nervous when he moved. That his hair was so orange that I expected it to crackle. That after he'd poked his fingers through it it was like little flames shooting up from his head. I wanted to praise his pragmatic attitude and compliment his manners. I wanted the interview to be a tribute.'

'If you can say all this to me, why couldn't you say it on paper?'

She got on to her knees beside him, unable to hide the intense small smile that kept playing about her mouth. 'Is that the kind of thing you enjoy reading?'

'That's the kind of thing a *lot* of people enjoy reading.' Jay gave her a quizzical look. 'Alex, what are you—— ?'

'Doing?' she finished for him. She wound her arms around his neck. 'I'm kissing you.'

And she did...very thoroughly, exulting when his mouth opened beneath hers, loving the way his beard rubbed scratchy-soft against her skin. When the kiss ended she was lying across Jay's chest and he was lying on his back. His breathing had gone awry. 'I'll have to say I've never known a woman to take criticism as well as you do.'

'You don't understand.' Alex caught his lean face between her hands and stared down with a feeling of absolute giddiness. 'It was all in there, Jay. Everything we've talked about was in my story on Dean. Robert cut it. He called it sentimental rubbish. He reduced a three-page interview which just might have been the best thing I ever wrote down to one page...with two extra photos.' She closed her eyes briefly. 'Sometimes I thought he'd cut my heart out with that red pen...piece by piece.' Realising how melodramatic that must have sounded, she added in a flat, concise tone, 'Robert believed in fact sheets.'

'And your uncle?' Jay questioned after a moment. 'He's running the magazine now. How does he feel?'

'Satisfied with the current formula.' Alex sighed and rubbed her face against his shoulder. 'It *is* working, you know... at least, for everyone except me. I did the O'Brien interview months ago, Jay. That was the last assignment I completed for Robert... the last assignment I completed, period. Uncle Stuart has been quite stoic about my writer's block,' she admitted stiffly. 'I think he'd just as soon see me give up. Then he and the cousins could have full control.' She lifted her head, misery apparent. 'Now do you understand why I didn't call myself a journalist?'

'Maybe you need a change,' Jay suggested quietly. 'There are other magazines.'

'But none of them belonged to my grandfather.' Her eyes stung unexpectedly. 'We were close—maybe not in the traditional grandparent-grandchild way, but in our own way. He made me feel smart and talented and capable of anything, and here I am, falling apart. He would expect better from me. *I* expect better from me. But I'm scared. It's as if I've suppressed my creative impulses so often in the name of format that I've started to just feel *dead* inside.' She wiped her face on the hem of her shirt and sat up. 'I think that was why this story seemed so important... it was exciting to *be* excited, you see?'

'I believe I do.' Jay sat up too, and, curving an arm about her rib-cage, drew Alex between his thighs. His chest felt solid against her back, his strong arms supporting her body in an embrace that was more comforting than seductive—at least for now.

Alex leaned her head against his shoulder, revelling in the tenderness, watching rain patter on the rocks outside.

'What will I do?' she asked after a time, and Jay sighed.

'I can't tell you that, sweetheart.' His lips brushed her temple. 'But, from what I can see, it comes down to a choice: either you're true to your grandfather's expectations, or you're true to yourself.'

'You were true to your family,' she reminded him bleakly.

'No.' He held her tighter, his fingers a warm pressure beneath her breast, his mouth against the side of her neck now, making her pulses thrum. 'I was lucky. For me, both options turned out to be the same.'

CHAPTER EIGHT

LAURA had stopped by after school and now stood on the lawn, examining the new leaves on one of Ty's many trees. She wore a pink shirt with cream trousers and espadrilles, her black hair pulled into its usual twist. 'I can't remember when I've seen a more gorgeous day!'

Alex smiled a response and wiped the back of one arm across her damp forehead. Her skin itched from contact with various weeds and her jeans were soiled from half sliding down the bank, but the weather was so fine that she didn't care. She emerged happily from the drainage ditch with a bouquet of wild daisies in her hands. 'Isn't it odd the places pretty things will grow? Let's take these inside, Laura, and I'll make some coffee.'

'I'd love to,' Jay's mother declared, 'but there's a PTA meeting after supper. I just stopped by to bring you something.' She dipped a hand into her shoulder-bag and withdrew a clutch of black and white photos. 'These pictures turned up when I cleaned the attic on Saturday. I thought you might like to have them.'

'How nice!' Shifting the daisies all to one hand, Alex took the photographs and immediately dimpled at the shot on top. She now recognised Ty's shy grin. And there was certainly no mistaking the doll-like girl who perched on his lap in Laura's porch swing. Elise had flashed a demure smile for the camera, but Ty looked halfway disconcerted... as if he couldn't decide what to do with his hands.

'That was taken one weekend at the farm.' Smelling subtly of lavender, Laura leaned over Alex's shoulder.

'The next one was taken here, though... after Ty and Elise had moved in. There seems to have been quite a time lapse between photo sessions.'

'So I see.' No wonder Elise had posed alone for this shot—her husband could barely have fitted in the camera's sights. Alex contemplated her mother's huge abdomen and thought, childlike, That was me. Then gradually the background shifted into focus and she began to pale and her hand shook so badly, holding the photos, that the final one sailed unheeded to the ground.

'What is it, Alex?' She didn't answer—couldn't—and Laura quickly got an arm around her waist. 'You're as white as a ghost!'

'I feel as if I've seen one,' Alex managed thinly. Daisies scattered, unnoticed. With her right hand she held out the picture of Elise. 'Look at this room.'

Laura's black eyes barely touched the photo before returning to Alex's stricken face. 'Granted, Ty let things go after your mother left,' she said, baffled, 'but it is the same place.'

'That's just the point.' Alex felt positively faint. 'It's exactly the same place! It can't be... but it is.' She saw Laura struggling to understand her agitation. She realised that she was not making sense. But then, how did one account for a happening that had no rational explanation? 'Could you come inside with me?' Her eyes were dark with panic. 'Please... just for a moment.'

Once they were inside the house Laura took the photograph back for a closer look. It was all there... the white linen on the bed, the ruffled curtains, the glazed milk pitcher full of flowers. Alex had exactly duplicated her mother's room... right down to the way she'd rearranged the furniture! 'I see what you mean,' Laura said quietly. When Alex sank into a kitchen chair she followed suit, reaching across the scrubbed pine table to gently squeeze the girl's trembling hands. 'What I don't understand is why you're frightened.'

'Because it's impossible. Don't you see that? I was ten months old when I left here.' She recounted her first look at the house and its haunting familiarity... the episode with Ty's pipe. Afterwards she sat staring across the small space, the skin around her mouth pinched white. 'Things like this don't really happen.'

'Things like this happen all the time,' Laura disagreed. 'Sometimes there's a logical explanation and sometimes...' she hesitated as if searching for words '...well, I prefer to think there's a spiritual explanation. And before you decide that I'm completely off my rocker,' she suggested composedly, 'will you hear me out?'

Alex nodded, and she slowly sat back in her chair. 'When you're married to a man for almost thirty years,' she presently stated, 'he becomes a part of you. Jason was more than a husband. He was my best friend, my confidant. When I lost him I thought my life was over. It was more than I could bear.

'Then one night I heard his favourite chair creak—the same way it had creaked for years each time Jason had settled into it—and maybe it was nothing more than an old spring giving way, I don't know. But that sound...that creaking chair helped me believe that Jason was near. That he'd always be with me.'

Her black eyes shone with emotion. 'For the first time in weeks I felt comforted. There were so many things I wanted to tell him, Alex. And I came to realise, that night, that there was nothing stopping me.

'Mind you, Jason's never *answered*,' a trace of humour tempered the poignant words, 'but who's to say that he doesn't hear? Who's to say,' she threw out softly, 'that Ty couldn't hear? If you believe, as I do, that the spirit of a person never dies then nothing is impossible.'

Alex shook her head. In spite of the enormous respect she felt for Laura, she could not accept what she was hearing. She was not ready for this. 'I think it's more than possible that I'm losing my mind.'

'That's nonsense,' Laura responded comfortably. 'Anyone in your position would be overwhelmed. You just need time. Time to fit the past into your life.'

Alex was not so easily reassured. She felt restless for days afterwards, as if some powerful force was at work, undermining her sense of reason, confusing chance with providence until she almost believed what Laura had said.

A spiritual explanation.

She imagined Ty looking down on her... projecting his gentle wisdom from a greater plane. Warmth flickered behind her eyes and disappeared, for immediately on the heels of that thought came the memory of Robert, who had hated such notions. Robert's standards for personal behaviour had matched his writing requirements. He had expected Alex to be smart, practical, and free of romanticism of any kind. She could not imagine Robert communicating from the grave.

Ty, though, had been a different man. An amazingly sensitive human being. A listener, Jay had said. But a man who had allowed his hands and his actions to speak for him freely.

So what are you trying to show me now?

Alex paced about, drawn yet dismayed by her own thoughts. She fiddled with the curtains and flicked at bits of dust, and finally fell backwards across her bed. The ceiling could use some help, she noted inconsequentially. In spite of her thorough cleaning, the wood beams were dark to the point of blackness and needed lightening.

The magazines that she'd bought upon her arrival were in the nightstand drawer, and she got them out, sporadically flipping through the pages in search of a photo that had caught her eye. There. She found the page and studied it from all angles, then let the book drop.

Eyes back on the ceiling, she whispered dispiritedly, 'Is this why you brought me here, Ty? To spruce up the place? Because that's all I've actually accomplished. That and——' her mouth softened '—meeting the nicest man alive.' Not that Ty would have meant to play matchmaker, she supposed. But when it came down to the wire she really couldn't know what he'd meant. That was the problem.

'If you wanted to come between Robert and me,' she whispered, 'then you're too late.' But, judging from the things she'd learned about Ty Conway, he had not been a man for vindictiveness. 'Was it to right an injustice, then? To show me the truth?'

She remembered Ty as he was in that third photo—the one she'd rescued from the yard. He wore a tender grin on his face while Alex, cradled in his arms, wore only a nappy. She was six or seven months old, at best, a tiny little thing with white hair and only two teeth, but clearly her father's pride and joy. She imagined him coming home from the fields a few weeks later. Finding no wife to greet him. No baby. His loneliness seemed to span time, to touch her, and her eyes filled. 'But you were young,' she whispered bleakly. 'You could have started over... started a new family. You didn't have to wait for us.'

She stopped and pressed both hands to her eyes, shaken by what she'd just said. Instinct told her it was true. Ty *had* waited. He had never given up hope. In his own passive way he had shown her more devotion than any of the people who had played a more active role in her life. 'Is that what you're trying to tell me, then? That you were always with me in spirit? That you still are?'

She lay quiet for a long time, listening to the wind and wondering what she'd expected to happen. A tear trickled into her hairline, and she asked wearily, 'Are you listening?' Her magazine slid to the floor, but she was exhausted and didn't bother retrieving it. 'If you're out there,' she bargained softly, 'could you give me a sign? Creak a chair, or something?'

There was just the wind, and then finally Alex's voice murmuring wistfully, 'Daddy?' But nothing happened, and, flinging an arm up over her eyes, she slept.

A few hours later she came wide awake and groped for the lamp. She pulled out the nightstand drawer in her haste to find pencil and paper, but it didn't matter. Nothing mattered except the urge to record her dream, and she hunched over the notebook, filling page after page, until her pencil lead went dull and her mind went blank.

She felt light-headed by the time she stumbled into the bathroom to wash, her hand cramped from voraciously scrawling across paper. Later she would read over what she'd written, but just now she wanted coffee, strong and black.

Her stiff fingers made kindling the fire a clumsy task, and she had to clutch the coffee-pot hard over the sink. She cranked the pump handle a couple of times to send water rattling into its enamelled metal bottom. Then she glanced up and gasped with wonder, and, for all her earlier efforts, let the coffee-pot clamber into the bowl.

The kitchen window was full of blossoms! She ran to the front door and saw a riot of pink in the yard, pink everywhere, pink flowers on every last tree! Ty's lawn had become a paradise!

Alex flew out on to the porch and, heart in her mouth, beheld the gorgeous sweep of colour. She barely noticed the chill boards beneath her bare feet, the dewy grass, as she revelled in the scene before her.

Twenty-two years of birthday gifts from her father!

Spirits soaring, throat salty, she flitted from tree to tree, touching the five-petalled flowers... breathing their delicate scent and weeping a little for the living tribute she'd been paid.

Then somehow, without even thinking about it, she stood on Jay's porch.

When he opened the door she held out a small perfect branch in both hands like an offering, her face still tear-streaked, but glowing. 'The dogwoods bloomed!'

'So I see.' Grinning faintly, Jay brushed a bent knuckle across her cheek. His eyes crinkled, travelling lazily up and down. 'In a hurry to tell me, were you?'

Alex glanced down, too, astonished to see that she was still in her nightdress. The white cotton covered her decently, though, almost to her ankles, and she found that this feeling—this impossible heartfelt wonder—had no link with practicalities. Jay was barely decent himself in faded jeans and nothing else, and she smiled back mistily. 'Yes. Aren't you going to kiss me hello?'

'You'd better believe it!' he growled, and pulled her into his arms. The kiss reflected a week's impatience, urgent and deliciously rough. When it ended Jay held Alex against his bare chest and stared down speculatively. 'So—what's got you so excited? Not that I'm complaining,' he insisted. 'I'm just wondering if it's something I should remember for the future.'

'I don't think so.' Alex dimpled and pulled away. 'This is a once-in-a-lifetime thing. My own private miracle.' She ran water at the sink and propped the dogwood branch in a tall glass. 'Trust me, it can't be duplicated.'

'That's too bad. Are you going to tell me the rest?'

She placed the glass in the centre of his table and then leaned against the counter-top to study it. A block of morning sunlight fell just so across the branch, casting its shadow. The room was awash with pale gold. Jay's eyes gleamed golden, too. He moved in front of her, dampness on his hair and beard from the shower, one eyebrow quizzically raised, and she warned softly, 'You'll think I'm a loon.'

'You don't sound particularly worried about it.' He trailed a slow fingertip down her cheek, murmuring in a husky tone, 'You look so incredible. Radiant. Even your eyes are glowing.' Alex smiled rather tremulously and lifted her mouth, but the kiss was brief. 'Tell me,' Jay coaxed.

'I don't know how to say it.' She hesitated, still smiling, then confided, 'Ty made the dogwoods bloom for me.' She saw Jay's eyebrow lift even further and amended wistfully, 'Well, OK, maybe he didn't. But you have to understand the way I felt last night.'

'How, baby?'

'Hopeless. As if there was no meaning to any of this. As if I'd never know him or know what he felt. And, without that, hadn't he just torn up my life for no reason? So I was lying in bed,' she recounted softly, 'and I told him. All of it. Then I said, "If you're listening, Ty, could you give me a sign?" And when I woke up,' her eyes shone, 'the dogwoods were in bloom. I know Ty really didn't make it happen, but he did plant the trees for me—and don't you think it's a lovely coincidence?'

'Yes, I do,' Jay agreed. He put a hand on either side of her head, fingers tangling in silken softness. 'And I'm all for anything that makes you this happy.'

'I feel as though I could fly!' Then a wave of emotion overcame her and her smile faded. 'There's no one else I could have told,' she said intensely.

'It's OK, little loon, your secret's safe with me.'

'I know.' Alex felt a new rush of warmth. She nuzzled her cheek into the curve of his palm and then kissed the slightly rough skin there, a soft little catch in her voice as she ventured for the first time, 'I think that's why I love you so much. You're very honourable.'

Jay went completely still for a moment. Then his hands slid deliberately to her waist, and with smiling lights in his eyes, devilment rasping his voice, he drawled, 'You think so?' Alex gasped when he lifted her on to the counter-top. Levering his body between her thighs, he linked his hands in the small of her back and pulled her closer. With their heads level and his breath fanning cleanly across her face he challenged, 'Look me in the eye and say that again.'

'I love you,' Alex whispered fervently.

She had no time to elaborate. Jay's mouth covered hers, sweet and hot, and desire filled her—desire mixed with an impossible buoyancy of spirit. Her fingers dug into the muscled flesh of his back. Her body strained close, deepening the already intimate kiss, and her limbs began to shake. A wondrous, heavy warmth spread in her abdomen... almost like pain.

Jay groaned low in his throat. Alex boldly slid her hips to the edge of the counter and let her slender thighs cradle him, savouring his unmistakable response. Fine tremors shuddered through him and his arms tightened. His breath turned ragged, his mouth devouring hers so fully that she went weak, but he made no move to go further.

Was he leaving it up to her, then? Still hungrily meeting Jay's kiss, shaking with intensity but very sure, Alex eased her shoulders back. She unbuttoned the bodice of her gown and drew his hand inside, feeling her breasts swell achingly to his touch. Her breath grew shallow and she moaned softly in her throat, urging him on, until finally he freed her mouth and took her breast instead.

The sight of his dark head nuzzled against her was too much! Wanting everything, wanting to give him everything, she caught his hand and guided it downwards...

'*Alex.*' His head came up and his lean fingers tangled with hers almost as if to ward her off. 'This may feel like teenager stuff, sweetheart,' his breath was laboured, 'but I'm not a teenager any more.'

'Neither am I.' Her blue-grey eyes were clear, solemn. She laid her free hand against his cheek, feeling the heat of his skin, the fine sheen of perspiration, and offered softly, 'We could go upstairs.'

'Yes, we could.' His voice was nowhere near steady. 'I could take you to bed and do everything I wanted to do that first night.'

Alex's blood beat wildly. 'Why don't you?'

'I will,' Jay promised darkly, 'soon.' He drew her tight into his arms again when she stiffened, resting his forehead against her temple with a muttered groan. 'Trust me, honey. Now isn't the best time. You're in this incredible mood because of Ty and it's made you very...generous towards me.' He paused, his voice rueful and low. 'So generous that I'm going half crazy wanting you. But it's no good if you regret it afterwards.'

'You mean you're saving me from my own impulsiveness?'

'Something like that.'

Alex arched back a bit, staring into his eyes, finding him darkly torn and not nearly as controlled as he might like her to think. A passionate kiss, an intimate touch, and his noble stand would crumble. Instinctively she knew. And her eyes filled. 'You're unreal,' she said softly. 'Do you know that?'

His gaze narrowed. 'You mean a real man would take what's offered?'

'No, that's not what I mean.' She placed a hand on either side of his face, her fingertips unconsciously tracing cheekbone and jaw. 'Oh, I'm so shaken up that I don't know what I mean! It's just that I've been turned down twice by the same man... well, three times if you count the night we met. And I think that rather makes my... condition your responsibility. So tell me, Mr Wise and Wonderful,' she said in a small, husky voice, 'what do we do at this point?'

'We re-focus.' He produced an endearing wry grin, still cradling her close. 'Find some mundane task to do.'

Alex moved lightly against him. 'Like making more coffee?'

'Right.' Fresh passion flared in his eyes and he took one last rather fierce kiss before disentangling himself with obvious and gratifying reluctance. 'Coffee,' he repeated drily. 'And maybe we'd better cook breakfast too.'

They were dining on buttered toast and Laura's strawberry preserves, the dogwood spray for a centrepiece, when Alex thought of another mundane task to do.

By mid-morning they had completed the necessary run to Joe's Hardware and were back at Ty's house, plaster dust-sheets liberally swathing furniture and floor. Jay stood on the bottom rung of a step-ladder, whitewashing the ceiling while Alex happily supervised. 'You missed a spot.' She pointed out a small zigzagged line where the light stain had not penetrated. 'To your left.'

'Bossy little thing, aren't you?' Jay wiped sweat from his brow with one forearm. Staring down, he smiled faintly at the way she looked, hair caught in a ribbon on top of her head, small feet bare. The old T-shirt he'd lent her fell nearly to her knees, outlining her slight curves while protecting the jeans underneath. His eyes grew dark watching her. Huskily, unconvincingly, he drawled, 'I feel sorry for the poor guy who ends up toeing your line.'

Melting a little, she watched him make another pass with the brush. 'There's a metal fastener in the wood,' he informed her. 'The paint won't adhere.'

Alex peered speculatively overhead. About ten inches along the same board she saw a similar fastener. There were four in all, joining two lengths of wood together. She would never have noticed them without the white paint as highlighter, but now that she saw them they didn't seem to fit. Guided by some unnamed hunch, she asked, 'What happens if you push against those boards?'

'I get paint on my hand,' Jay groaned. 'Come on, honey. Have a heart.' But her imploring gaze proved too much for him. With a resigned sigh, he pushed.

At first nothing happened. Then old dirt sprinkled on to the dust-sheet protecting her bed and, as the boards gave way, fine debris dislodged also. Jay peered into the dusty opening. 'Looks like a makeshift access door.' Wiping paint-slick fingers down his jeans, he thoughtfully met her eyes. 'I could use a flashlight, if you have one.'

Alex took the paintbrush he held out and rested it haphazardly on the rim of the pail. Then she searched through the nightstand drawer to produce a tiny penlight. 'How's this?'

'Great.' Jay switched on the light, and, using one elbow for leverage, eased his head and shoulders into the attic. 'There isn't much up here,' he immediately ascertained. 'Just a couple of boxes.'

Within seconds he had handed down the first—an old shoe box tied with cord. Alex took it gingerly, half leery of a mouse or something worse rustling out. But as soon as she sank on to the bed and unwound the string she forgot to be wary. The box contained letters—dozens of them. The elegant stationery was familiar, the handwriting unmistakable. Shaken, Alex lifted her head. 'They're from my mother.'

Jay found an old rag to wipe his hands. Then he sat next to Alex and slowly thumbed through the envelopes. All were of similar design...feminine, expensive, faintly redolent of perfume. The scent rose to Alex's nostrils, and for a moment she felt as if Elise stood beside her. Jay's slight frown brought her back to earth and she asked uncertainly, 'Do you...should I read them?'

He slid an arm around her, massaging her opposite shoulder. 'I don't know,' he said gravely. 'If there's a chance they might answer your questions then I don't think Ty would mind. But are you sure you want to?'

Alex shivered lightly. 'It isn't a question of wanting.'

She was grateful for his reassuring hand on her shoulder as she fumbled open the first envelope. A photo from her third birthday party immediately fluttered to the floor. Leaving Jay to retrieve it—and to smile over it—she scanned the first paragraph, which effected a stilted and strained apology from Elise to Ty. Then the tone of the letter changed and Alex drew in her breath. Haltingly she began to read aloud.

'...impossible to believe that Alexandra is three. Robert had his secretary buy her an enormous doll dressed in lace and ribbons, but he didn't attend the party.'

Sensing Jay's eyes on her, she felt compelled to explain, 'He was too busy. Every year they'd give me a big, beautiful present to open with his regrets. I came to expect it, really.' She stared down at her hands gripping the page, and shrugged. 'Some days I would have traded every toy I owned for a couple of hours of his time.'

The sentiment was bitterly echoed in her mother's next words.

'He thinks his money should be enough for us. Isn't that ironic? I left you because I couldn't live without money. Now I have money, and no life. I've made such a miserable mess of things! I must see you, Ty. Robert is out of town next weekend. I'm bringing Alexandra to McGee.'

Something began to unfurl in Alex. A memory—milky and insubstantial, like one of the dream sequences she'd seen in films. She closed her eyes and the house seemed to change before her, shifting its proportions. The ceiling rose and the walls widened. Darkness filled the strange corners and a tall man's shadow stretched across the floor.

But, try as she might, she couldn't hold the image. A small sound escaped her, half-sigh, half-sob, and she felt Jay's arm tighten. With shaking hands she returned the letter to its envelope and opened another. A tender missive following the visit, its theme was consistent with two poignant lines: '"Alexandra adored you as I adore you. How could I have been so wrong?"' Alex read that part to Jay, her reaction a bitter-sweet mix of regret and relief.

'If Mother brought me back here when I was three,' she said tautly, 'then there's no mystery in my knowing this house. Small children can form lasting impressions where babies can't.'

Her theory was to be strengthened by another message, short and starkly to the point.

I can't risk bringing Alex to see you again. She almost gave us away last night when Robert lit a cigar. 'Make smoke like the nice man, Daddy,' she said. These days I can't bear her calling him Daddy...but what else can I do? Alex is accustomed to this house. She has ballet lessons and a nanny, the prettiest clothes and the best toys...anything she wants. If I leave Robert she loses everything. I simply can't do it. At least, not yet.

Had those words really been written with a three-year-old in mind? Alex could sympathise with the maternal plea... but only to a point. It would be difficult... extremely difficult to choose near-poverty over wealth for one's child. But surely personal happiness meant more than possessions?

And how had Ty felt when he'd read this page?

Alex paled, knowing that her imagination could not define his pain. To be given back his lost child, only to have her snatched away! To be offered Elise's love, but on the most shallow of terms. And, worst of all, to be cruelly reminded of his shabbiness in her eyes. He must have felt worthless. Degraded.

She finished the letter and, trembling, offered it to Jay. But he grimly shook his head. 'No, honey. You have a right to read it. I don't.' He searched her eyes for a moment. 'Tell me later, if you want.'

Alex nodded, watching him pick up the paintbrush again, wondering how he could calmly work when she felt this way, more disillusioned with every line she read...

She realised, finally, why Ty had waited. Each letter contained the same poignant phrases: 'Some day...when Alex is older...I'll tell her, darling...we'll be together then.' The promises were essentially empty ones. Alex could see that now. But mightn't Ty had been blinded by his love and loyalty to the point of allowing himself to believe? She imagined him existing for months at a time on false hope. Clinging to the assurances of the latest letter while Elise clung to her role in his life, refusing to be forgotten.

She was stunned to find a piece she'd written tucked inside one of the last envelopes. It was quietly passionate—an indictment of people who misused their power. She'd penned it in high school and it could have been inspired by anyone... the principal, her journalism teacher, Robert. Elise wrote with an equal but different passion, 'She is so like you, Ty. Robert tries to kill it, to weed it out... but your spirit prevails.'

Alex shivered, wondering at the paradox.

Then she came to the final letter, postdated less than two weeks before the accident. Its tone was sadly reminiscent... almost as if Elise had known.

> How I've misled you. Making promises I couldn't honour. Talking of the future. We never had a future, did we? If only I could start over, my life would be so very different. Yours, too, my sweet, faithful Ty. And Alexandra's... I wish to God that I had told her.

'So do I, Mother,' Alex whispered.

She carefully replaced the envelopes and tied up the cord, then rose from the bed, surprised to find that her body had stiffened. Jay's ladder was in the far corner now; he'd almost finished the ceiling. She was unaware that he had joined her until she stood at one of the front windows and felt his chest come up solid against her back. His arms slid about her waist, but she remained stiff within their circle.

'I could have forgiven her for leaving him.' Her voice drifted to him, strained, scarcely audible. 'I was prepared to excuse her for that. I mean, if they were incompatible... if she was unhappy, marriage didn't have to mean a life sentence, right? But she wanted it both ways. She wanted Ty on reserve, like a... a spare tyre that you patch and throw back in the trunk for emergencies. She wanted her place held.'

Jay sighed, his breath gently stirring her hair. 'I doubt her place was ever up for grabs, Alex. Ty loved her. In his eyes she never stopped being his wife.'

'But she should have stopped. That's the problem.' Alex caught the pink shimmer of dogwood blossoms through her tears. 'She should have had the decency to release him once and for all. Instead she kept him tied up and dangling. "I love you, but I can't be with you. I have to think of our daughter."' She dashed a hand across her cheek. 'Maybe that's why it hurts so much. She used me as an excuse to keep him in limbo.

'And Robert. I've been determined to blame him for everything.' She closed her eyes, a dozen fragmented scenes falling into place. The fights that had once gone over her head. Her mother's cruelty...which she'd always dismissed as self-defence. Robert's brooding silence. 'There was so much bitterness between them...I just assumed, somehow, that he was at fault. But Robert was an intelligent man, Jay. Why wouldn't he be bitter? Mother used him, too.

'She left Ty because he was poor, even though she loved him, and she stayed with Robert because he was wealthy, even though she despised him. And I keep thinking——' she drew a deep breath '—who was this woman? Because I didn't know her. Not really.'

'OK,' he murmured near her ear. 'OK, sweetheart.'

Miserable, Alex leaned against him. 'I thought I wanted to know the truth. Now I wish I'd left it alone. I'm sorry to be a part of it.'

'Don't,' he admonished huskily. 'You aren't to blame. Certainly not in Ty's eyes—and if you need proof of that,' he nodded towards the flowering trees, 'he left a legacy of his love for you right out there. There's no doubt in my mind that he only wanted the best for his daughter.'

'The best?' she repeated numbly. What was that? A big, lonely house full of hostile voices? Piano lessons and exclusive schools and an upper-class society with no stomach for backwoods men? 'Some people have a mistaken view of what's best.'

'Granted—and I'll be the first to tell you how much you missed, not knowing Ty. But there's something else you might consider,' Jay added sombrely. 'Suppose you'd grown up right here in Conway County? Suppose I'd seen you around all my life? You'd be like a little sister to me.' He bent his head and gently nuzzled her neck. 'There's no way I'd feel comfortable doing this.' He let his hand slide over her breast. 'Or this.'

Alex knew he was trying to coax a smile, but she couldn't seem to oblige. 'I'm sorry,' she said tensely. 'I can't just shrug this off.'

'Then don't shrug it off.' He patiently rested his chin atop her head. 'Talk about it.'

Alex sighed, a part of her conscious of Jay's body, of being cocooned in his arms. Another part of her hurt terribly. 'I don't know what to say,' she balked perversely.

'Then don't say anything.'

His adaptability accomplished what coaxing did not. Alex's mouth quirked. She brushed at a trailing tear and tipped her face backwards, staring upside-down into his gravely smiling eyes. 'Good advice,' she murmured, drawing courage from the warmth of his gaze. 'Maybe I'll go see what's in the other box.'

The carton felt quite heavy. Alex prised it open and found three old-fashioned binders—the schoolroom variety with covers made of cardboard and coarse blue cloth. She stared at the top one for a long moment, then finally she lifted it, her breath catching at the bulge of filled pages inside.

She began to read with trepidation. By the time she'd made it through the first leaf her heart was pounding and her mouth had gone dry. She'd never dreamed...never suspected. 'Oh, Ty,' she breathed, almost sobbing with wonder. Amazed and humbled, she flung up her head. 'You aren't going to believe this,' she got out shakily, her eyes shimmering, colliding with Jay's. 'My father was a writer.'

CHAPTER NINE

'A JOURNEY into the heart of Kentucky,' a critic would later tag the collection.

For Alex, that first reading was a journey into the soul of Ty Conway. A man of insight and deep emotion, he had filled his work with tenderness, poetry, wisdom and humour. His reflections on God and man moved her, his short stories caught her imagination, and his thumbnail personality sketches made her smile. And always, interwoven with every theme, she sensed his reverence for the Kentucky hills, his love for home.

Expecting gentle stories from a gentle man, Alex caught glimpses of fire instead. Indian figures dominated his work, responding even more cleverly to ink than they had to wood. Ty showed a passion for his cause... leading Alex to understand what her mother had meant. 'She is so like you, Ty. Robert tries to kill it, to weed it out.'

Ty, too, wrote with his heart.

She felt a shiver of pride and cognizance while reading his short poem 'Daisy in a Ditch'. On a surface level the verse symbolised beauty within harsh surroundings, the survival of pure ideals in a corrupt world. Then a parallel struck her—the transplanted orchid, refusing to thrive—and she realised that Ty was not without his dark side.

But what a marvellous talent! Hadn't he known? Her heart ached with loss for him, her imagination relentlessly rounding out the picture until she saw him clearly... humble, torn with insecurities, his self-worth crippled by the woman he loved. Elise had called him nobody, and he'd believed her. One cruel act of rejection and the limits had been set.

Never had poetic justice been so clear. With his wife's support Ty might have found the courage to submit a story or a poem. He might have been discovered and honoured by the literary community for his splendid work, the end result being a better life—a nice home, fine clothes, a few of the luxuries Elise had found so necessary. He might have made her happy.

'Oh, Mother.' Alex pressed her forehead to the rough cloth binder. 'Look what you've done.'

Nothing was the same afterwards. All the roles had shifted for Alex. Her grandparents had become snobs...Robert a spurned husband and victim...her mother a disturbed woman whom she no longer knew. It was a shake-down of the characters who had built *her* character, and Alex came away shaken. She was unsure where she stood now. Perhaps she'd crumbled along with them.

Outwardly she went on with her life, found ways to keep busy. She cut the lawn with Ty's ancient push mower and weeded flowerbeds, wearing his old torn gloves. She scrubbed the front porch, and washed the outside windows. She took the step-side truck for a run, and almost died of embarrassment when it spluttered to a halt in the dead centre of the main road; to her great surprise Jake waived his tow bill, but charged her for the petrol, suggesting with a hateful grin that she check the fuel gauge next time.

She stuck to her own car afterwards, shopping with Meredith, running out to the farm. She baby-sat Adam one evening and fell in love, not only with him, but with the discovery that she was quite competent at caring for an infant when left to her own devices.

She borrowed cookery books from the library and planned elaborate weekend meals for Jay. And, all in all, she thought she was coping very well...

'What in the name of Sam Hill do you think you're doing?'

Alex raised her hoe again, breathing hard, reluctant to break the rhythm of her swing. There was something oddly cathartic about the planting of seeds in new ground; her level of concentration ran high.

Jay took a paralysing grip on the handle and she lifted her head. 'It's not a race!' he admonished. 'Slow down.' His displeasure startled her... though not half as much as her sudden perception of nightfall. The call of a lone whippoorwill shivered down her spine, waking a few thousand nerve-endings. Her back was killing her! She caught Jay's eyes again and her mouth tightened nervously at their expression; no point looking for sympathy there.

'What's the matter?' Her voice was shockingly insubstantial. Just forming the words drained her. She had been functioning on a different plane, her body a smooth machine, her mind on stand-by.

He released the hoe, but kept his hand close to ensure that she didn't resume. 'Suppose you tell me?'

'Isn't it...obvious?' Irritation flared, then lost impact to her struggle for breath. The subtle little cut came out cut to pieces. 'I'm planting...a...garden.'

'I got that part. How long have you been out here?'

'I don't know.' The sun had been fairly high when she'd started. Now only pink streaks coloured the west. She tabulated quickly and decided that her maths couldn't be right. 'A couple...of hours.'

'A couple of *days*, from the looks of you!' Alex opened her mouth to protest, but his deep frown silenced her. 'And don't talk! Just stand there and get your breath, will you do that? Honestly, sweetheart, this doesn't make a whole lot of sense.'

He sounded distraught. The shaken note in his voice surprised Alex into an awareness of how she must appear. Her hair was plastered to her head in damp strings. The sun had been warm, the work very physical. Her clothes were damp, too. The night, though, was cooling, and as if on cue her body began to shiver. She suddenly felt more tired than she had ever been in her life. She had to fight to remain standing; she wanted nothing more than to sink into the soft ground at Jay's feet.

'What doesn't make sense?' There. A whole sentence without gasping.

'Everything.' Jaw tight, Jay scanned the ploughed square of earth with its neat rows. 'What possessed you to start a garden?'

What *had* possessed her? A whiff of freshly ploughed earth through an open window of her car. The thought of silking corn on a sultry summer afternoon... biting into a sun-warmed tomato and knowing she'd grown it with her own hands. Her need to dig in, to belong here. Avoiding the pathos, she said carefully, 'I like vegetables.'

'So what's wrong with the farmers' market? We only have weekends together after Monday. I haven't planned to spend them chopping weeds.'

'Oh.' Pressing a fist to the small of her back, Alex speculatively searched his face. He didn't know, of course. How could he? He'd been in Louisville all week, wrapping up his classes, packing up his things. She hadn't decided until yesterday. But his proprietorial attitude was nice. She held his eyes, breathing easier now, anticipating his reaction. 'I'm not going back on Monday.'

Emotion flickered over his face, too quick to be read. He shifted stance as if to brace himself, pushed his hands deeper into his pockets.

He wore his jeans remarkably well, Alex thought numbly. His height, too, always amazed her. She studied his navy open-collared shirt, his white athletics shoes. Garden soil had settled like a film on the expensive leather. 'Is that wise?' he asked while she was still staring at his shoes. 'You've already taken two extra weeks.'

Alex angled her chin, unaware that the move bespoke defiance. 'I called Uncle Stuart again. He's not in the least opposed to extending my leave. Things are going fine without me.'

Jay's eyes narrowed. 'He said that?'

'No. He said "take all the time you need", but I can read between the lines as well as anyone. And—to tell you the truth—I'm relieved. There are some things I want to do.'

'Really? Like what?'

Alex caught his meaning, and her mouth took on an unhappy slant. 'Like none of your business.' She flung a pointed look towards the house. 'I'm going inside to clean up.'

'Alex, wait a second.' When she kept walking Jay made an exasperated sound and followed her. 'I'm just trying to get some answers, sweetheart. What are you afraid of?'

'Not a thing,' she insisted flatly, framed now by the doorway. 'Wipe your feet if you're coming inside, will you?'

Jay gave her a speaking glance, but paused on the porch to knock loose soil from his shoes. Alex had just enough time to consider the mess she'd left. Then he was there beside her, grimly surveying the wrecked room.

Flour covered the kitchen table and much of the floor—a by-product of her first batch of home-made bread. The refrigerator stood in a puddle of water, its door propped back with a chair. And cut flowers lay wilting on the draining board. *'Oh.'* A drooping sprig of hyacinth condemned her. 'I forgot to put them in water!' Disconcerted, she blurted out, 'I was defrosting the refrigerator while I waited for the dough to rise—only the ice took so long to melt that I decided to gather some flowers. Then John Shawn came with the tractor...' She broke off, biting her lip. 'You think I'm hopeless, don't you?'

Jay studied the loaves that had risen, ready to be baked. 'I think that looks like good bread,' he said evenly. Then his eyes came level, holding hers with a directness she didn't like. 'I also think you're trying very hard to be something you're not.'

'You mean domesticated?'

'No, content.'

Alex's throat tightened. She moved away from him, crossing to the kitchen sink to pump water over her hands. 'I'm not going to listen to this.'

'Oh, yes, you are,' he said grimly. 'I want to know what you're trying to prove. Do you mean to hibernate indefinitely, stirring up batter and chopping corn?'

'Maybe.' She dried her hands, then found a container and began filling it with water. 'It's a pretty nice existence. I wish my mother had tried harder to appreciate that. She might have ruined a few less lives.'

Jay exhaled slowly and took a step towards her. 'Is that what this is all about? Proving you're a better woman than she was? You can't compensate for your mother's shortcomings, Alex.'

Putting the stems into water, she plucked at a bloom or two, then lowered her hands to the edge of the sink, gripping it tightly. 'I'm staying for the summer,' she told him in a taut voice. 'If you don't want me around then say so, but don't start analysing. I'm not in the mood.'

'Then you'd better get in the mood——' Jay grasped her shoulders and dragged her to face him '—because I'm not leaving until we've settled a thing or two!' He gave her a little shake for emphasis, inadvertently jarring stressed muscles so that she whitened. Biting off a rude expletive, he ground out harshly instead, 'If I thought you were happy it would be different. But look at you! You're exhausted. You're trembling. What are you *doing* to yourself?'

'Making a life,' she came back in a flat tone. 'At least that's what I *thought* I was doing.' Emotion blazed in her eyes. She felt trapped suddenly, hemmed up in a corner. 'I had this crazy idea that we might spend the summer together. You know? Swim in the river. Go fishing. Eat water-melon. Maybe sit in your mother's porch swing.'

A muscle pulsed along his jaw. 'That sounds idyllic, but——'

'No, thanks? Fine. I should have consulted you.'

'Will you shut up?' Jay thrust a hand under her chin, searching her face, his expression one of angry frustration. 'It sounds idyllic,' he repeated tautly, 'except for one thing. Where does your writing fit in?'

The fire in Alex died. She wrenched away from him and went to the refrigerator, blindly grabbing a mop from behind it. The puddle looked two inches deep; she'd be sopping at it all night.

'I asked a question, Alex. What about your writing?'

'What writing?' she retorted and set to work. Within moments, though, his fist had surrounded the mop handle and the cotton head of it sloshed to a halt. Alex watched ripples form on the floor. 'I have to clean this up.' She raised her head, her mouth a thin, stubborn line. 'Wood doesn't take to standing water.'

'So that's your answer?' he grated, ignoring her. 'You're copping out? Denying your talent? Evading the issue?'

'Don't talk to me about evasion!' Alex reacted. 'This is the first little bit of peace I've seen since the day I discovered my talent—and I'm using the term loosely since I'm no longer sure it exists, or whether it ever did. A person's gift shouldn't make them miserable.'

'No,' he agreed, 'it shouldn't.' He took the mop out of her hands and propped it against the wall. 'But look how many people have bent your gift to fit their purposes.'

'I don't want to discuss this. You know nothing about it.'

'I know what you've told me,' he insisted. 'I know how your grandfather picked you out of the group. He made you his protégé, encouraged you, right? But he expected a lot in return. You had to do things his way— that was the price of his approval—and a lot of good it did either of you, because he died before you were old enough to be given any power.

'So the job goes to Robert,' he stubbornly continued. 'Here's a man, I'll wager, who bitterly resented his father-in-law's authority. He's in control now, and anyone who can't adjust can darn well leave—including his daughter, who, bravely, I think, decides to stay and make a go of it. You were young, Alex. Still finding your feet. And yet you had to forget everything Bannon taught you and re-learn the business Robert's way——'

'You make him sound heartless!'

'Wasn't he?'

'No.' She backed away from him, hugging her arms across her chest, her small face rigid. 'I used to think so. But not any more. I... there's something I promised to tell you about Robert.' She caught his gaze, clung to it. 'Do you remember asking me once why I called him by his first name?' Jay nodded, and she jerkily imparted, 'I was twelve, and I'd written a Father's Day poem for him, which I read aloud over dinner. When I finished Mother leaned across the table with tears in her eyes. "You remind me so much of your father," she told

me. "He used to write poetry, too." I thought she meant Robert. I turned to him, unbearably excited, and said, "Did you really, Daddy? Could you show it to me?" He just stared at me, all funny and cold. Then he sent me to my room. I thought my poem wasn't good enough.' She bit her lip. 'Now I know better. Mother was talking about Ty's poetry. That's why Robert reacted the way he did.'

Jay gazed down at her, assimilating huskily, 'OK, honey. So Robert tried to make you more *his* daughter, and less Ty's... but if you can see his motivations then you should be able to break free of the restrictions he imposed on your writing.'

'*No,*' she came back again. 'Haven't you heard anything I said? I can't do it any more. I haven't a hope of measuring up to Ty. And I'd betray Robert just by trying... so what's the use? Either way I go, I let one of them down.'

'Of all the ridiculous...!' Jay caught her shoulders firmly, leaving her no choice but to meet his gaze, which was stern and terrible. 'Let me tell you something, Alex. Turn your back on your talent now and you've robbed Ty of his last chance to be a father to you.' Hands tightening on her arms, he added, low-toned, 'Not every example is meant to be followed, honey. Learn from Ty's mistakes, don't repeat them. Don't bury yourself up here.'

Her eyes darkened to turbulent grey. 'You think I should go back to work, don't you?'

Jay sighed. 'Back to work, yes. Not necessarily back to the company. I suspect your uncle has done everything in his power to help you out of the door. And, from what you've told me, the cousins are still harbouring a grudge—your grandfather saw to that when he played favourites. It doesn't sound like a healthy place.'

No, it wasn't healthy at all. It was cold, and hostile, and uncomfortable, and she realised with a shock that if she never saw her office again she'd lose no sleep—or at least no more than usual.

Good grief! She passed a hand over her face, and it was trembling. She'd come up here to find inner peace, and look at her! She was in worse shape now than on the day she'd arrived. No wonder Jay didn't want her to stay.

'Can we talk about this later?' she asked thinly.

'No, we can't.' He held her still, and for the first time she didn't enjoy her smallness or the feel of his body strong and hard against her. She wanted to escape—to cover her ears. 'If you think I'm going to stand by and watch you destroy yourself,' he continued severely, 'then you don't know me very well. Let's get that straight. And when are you going to face reality? You can't please everyone—it's impossible. You can't write to suit Grandpa Bannon and Ty and Robert. No—they're three different people. So you write to suit Alex.' His dark eyes roamed over her face, searching intensely. 'You do it your way.'

'You make it sound so easy!' she burst out in spite of herself. 'Can you tell me how?'

Jay's mouth settled into a firm line. 'The last thing you need is someone else telling you how. I'm certainly no writer—I won't attempt it. But I won't hinder the process, either.'

His mind was set, Alex realised. She felt helpless, stricken. 'Why don't you just say it?' she demanded wildly. 'You're determined to get rid of me!'

'Damn it... *no*.' That shocked her, because he rarely swore and now he'd done it twice in one night. Frustration got the better of him and he grasped her head, tipping her face to meet his mouth. The kiss was hard and vaguely bruising. Alex didn't enjoy it. Nor did she enjoy the way he looked at her afterwards, as if she had provoked him. 'You drive me crazy sometimes, do you know that?' His eyes were dark with strain. 'I'm not talking about forever, Alex. I just want you to take some time. Time away from me, us.'

'You flatter yourself if you think you're such a big distraction!' She felt no better for denying it. Jay *was* a distraction, so much so that she'd gladly make him the centre of her life—if he wanted the position, which he obviously didn't. 'I'm sorry,' she said miserably. 'I just—— What about my garden? I've planted it now. I stopped by Paula's office to pick up some pamphlets on home canning, and she gave me a recipe for tomato sauce——'

'Hang Paula!' Jay growled, running a hand through his hair. 'Look. I'll take care of the garden for you. I'll mow the grass. I'll even make the blasted tomato sauce if that's what it takes. Just go back and find yourself——' he grimaced over the trite phrase '—so we can be together. Will you do that, please, sweetheart?'

He reached out to touch her face, the gesture so final that Alex flinched. 'This is crazy! I'm not going anywhere!' Panic welled up tight in her throat, and against all her better judgement she pleaded strickenly, 'If you love me, Jay... if you care for me at all, you won't ask me to leave!'

His eyes darkened as if he'd like nothing better than to pull her into his arms, smooth away her insecurities like so many wrinkles in a wind-whipped sheet. But he didn't touch her. He stood where he was, his mouth a lean straight line that said none of the words she wanted to hear, and after a moment she jerkily pushed past him.

Humiliated, hurt, and trying desperately not to cry, she crossed the room and held open the door. 'Look. I'm tired. I still have bread to bake and this mess to clean up, and all I can think about is a hot bath. I don't mean to be rude——' she drew a long, ragged breath '—but will you please go home?'

'Honey.' He stopped in front of her, compassion deep in his eyes, and something hot inside Alex seemed to break.

'Don't!' she objected fiercely. 'Don't call me that. It doesn't mean anything now. It's just pity, and that's the last thing I want from you, Jay McGee! Oh...' She was furious, really shaking, and then suddenly his mouth was sliding across hers, heedless of coursing tears. His hand lifted her until she felt the door at her back, his body pressed close in front like a hard cradle of suspension, and it was the most exquisite sensation, being kissed in mid-air. Alex didn't want to respond. She wanted to writhe and kick and claw at his face, but the softness of his lips felt too good, the taut warmth of his body felt too right, and she kissed him back as she'd never kissed him before—she wanted him to remember her!

He intently watched her face afterwards, slowly sliding her body down his own, creating a deliberate friction. 'That wasn't pity,' he said with grave satisfaction. 'Pity is the last thing I'd offer you, Alex Stevens!' Then the faint humour faded and he searched her drowning eyes. 'You'd better come back,' he warned in a husky voice. 'If you don't I'll come after you, and I won't fight fair.'

Alex swallowed. 'Is that a promise?'

'No way,' Jay said succinctly. 'It's a threat.'

What now? she wondered as she rose, dripping, from the tub. Her skin was shrivelled and chilled. She'd lain there too long, brooding, letting the water grow cold. After she'd towelled off, though, she stepped before the mirror to comb her wet hair and realised that the soak had done her good. She didn't feel so crazy any more. An earlier glimpse of her face had shocked her! Eyes wild, cheeks tear-streaked and faintly marked with dirt, she had borne the appearance of someone who needed counselling. She'd made do with a strong self-lecture on the importance of perspective, but at least now her eyes didn't haunt her. They looked solemn. Grave.

She belted her terry robe about her waist and walked through the still house, guided by moonlight, touching this object or that. She straightened a picture, smoothed a pillow, and finally stood at the front window with her palm pressed to the cool glass. Out in the yard her dogwood trees were bathed in silver. By day, though, they had started to look forlorn, the blossoms discoloured and curling, petals sifting to the ground.

Jay was right. She'd outstayed her visit.

These last few weeks she'd been like a woman possessed. Gathering experiences. Heaping up country wisdom. Identifying with her father's life in an effort to repair her own. But it hadn't worked.

She let the curtain fall and paced across the room, then stopped. Hadn't she done enough pacing? What was she waiting for—a lightning bolt to strike and clear the confusion like so much haze on a humid day? Well, it wasn't going to happen—not like that, not without an effort on her part. Right again, Jay.

She flipped the main light switch, and with growing resolve dragged her suitcase from under the bed, groaning as her strained back knotted up. She had to remove Ty's clothes before she could pack her own, and her fingers lingered over his tweed coat. Childishly she brought it to her face, sniffed the rich odour of tobacco, and then blinked, furious at her own sentimental tears. This wasn't goodbye forever! Jay couldn't make her leave. She was going of her own free will and she would come back just as easily, whenever she pleased. It was her house, for heaven's sake!

Within a short while she had her blouses and trousers rolled, her sweaters folded, her underwear neatly piled on the bed. She'd bought some things since her arrival—shorts and tops for warmer weather, magazines, food—too much to fit in the suitcase, but there were paper sacks for the overflow and she'd manage.

She threw out the flowers and washed the vase, then organised the perishables to be packed first thing in the morning. Those mountain curves had been terrifying enough by daylight; scorned or no, Alex wasn't free falling through darkness! Not for Jay McGee or any man.

Weary, moving mechanically, she took a couple of framed photographs from the nightstand, wrapped them in tissue, and tucked the bundle for safety into one of her leather boots. The drawer itself didn't hold much. Her pen-light; the magazines, which she reserved in hopes of lulling herself to sleep; pencil and paper. Removing a spiral notebook, she flipped through it and noticed with mild interest that some of the pages were filled.

Turning backwards, she found a block of several pages, each covered in a black scrawl that she scarcely recognised as her own. Frowning, she sank down on the bed and distractedly began to read, but within moments her mouth had dried, her hands were shaking. She hadn't done this, surely? She hadn't *dreamt* this?

But it *was* her dream, running like a film screen through her mind, conveying lush scenery, ancient dense forests, a taste of grave danger constant in the air. She saw prehistoric men dwelling in the cliffs for protection, and one mighty untamed man who stalked the forest alone. Only the youngest daughter of the village chief had seen him. Attracted by his strength, drawn by his wildness, she set out to track him and snare his heart...

It was a powerful passage, but only that. Alex shivered nervously, wrestling with the unexpected conviction that it could be strengthened into something more.

Impulsively she dragged out Ty's binders and searched through them until she at last found the poem she wanted. Its four simple stanzas told of an Indian chief who had fought to keep his culture pure. He was not unlike Jay's desecrated warrior, nor was he so different from the red man in Alex's dream. Like them, he inevitably fell to opposing forces. But who, having read that poem, could dismiss his existence as just so many relics lying in a field?

She remembered her strange reaction to the Indian fort. She remembered, too, her trip to the rock house and the way Ty's carved maiden had shimmered to life before the fire. What had Jay said that morning? 'Write the story...who knows? Maybe you can open a few eyes.' Not long afterwards her subconscious had thrown her this curve, this dream, this great big neon clue—but she had been too preoccupied to grasp it.

She glanced over her scribbled pages again and found that a second reading did not diminish her excitement. The piece evoked a strong sense of stepping backwards in time. It was elemental, charged with stark imagery—and yes, worthy of expansion.

Ideas swirled through her brain, and she fell back against the pillows, biting her lip, hoping she wasn't wrong. She thought of the risks, the possibilities, and she felt dizzy. 'Fiction,' she whispered dazedly. She'd never seriously considered the genre, although on one inimical occasion Robert had shouted that she ought to be writing romance novels—she had the imagination for it.

The statement had been hurled as an insult and taken as such, but she felt curiously bolstered by it now. There were no guarantees, of course. She might be an abject failure. She might waste weeks or even months of her time before she knew. But at least she would be working on her own—intrigued and challenged. She would be pleasing Alex.

And, if she regained Jay's respect in the process, all the better!

CHAPTER TEN

ALEX stood before her sleek gas fireplace, a small scarlet figure in the elegant grey room, her hostess gown a swirl of silk, her perfume floating lavishly on the evening air. Her hair swung like a pearly cloud about her face. She looked feminine, alluring. Never mind that she was alone with no plans. She'd spent too many days in sweat-shirts and pony-tails! And, besides, she was celebrating.

Fresh excitement feathered along her spine. She lifted a delicate china cup to the three photographed faces on the mantel and offered a grave smile. 'To you, gentlemen,' she solemnly toasted the framed trinity, 'for your unique contributions to my new career. This accomplishment belongs to each of you.'

Her gaze swept the first likeness, and she studied the distinguished features, the silver hair and moustache, the clear pale blue eyes. 'Thank you, Grandfather,' she murmured simply, 'for believing in me. You were the first, and sometimes the only one who did.'

The centre portrait earned a longer pause. Alex grew wistful and solemn over the darkly handsome face, reaching—as he would have expected—for the right words. 'My gratitude, Robert, for your unrelenting requirement of my best. You taught me precision, structure, discipline, staying power. I'll never forget you,' she vowed. 'You've been a great influence in my life.'

'And then there's you, Ty.' Her voice softened; the final photograph, one of father and child, brought smiling lights to her eyes. 'You may not realise this, but you've certainly left your mark on the world! You're being published,' she imparted, savouring the words. 'They're calling you the next Jesse Stuart, a revelation, a state treasure. How does your mountain logic answer that?' she challenged with a proud grin. 'There must be an appropriate saying. How about "you can't keep a good man down"?'

Her throat caught unexpectedly and she swallowed as the gentle face shimmered before her eyes. 'Thank you, Daddy,' she tenderly whispered, 'for giving me back my heart. I hope, wherever you are, that the favour's been returned.'

The small ritual thus carried out, she sipped her coffee and breathed a troubled sigh. She was intensely aware of a fourth man who deserved her thanks. If Jay hadn't insisted that she confront her dream... if his ultimatum hadn't become the catalyst, then she might still be holed up at the cabin, letting bitterness choke her talent, watching it wither altogether.

'Only that didn't happen. I found myself. I found my calling.' The words echoed emptily round the room. What good was a celebration without Jay to share it? So she'd had her manuscript accepted. So she'd floated on clouds for most of the day. Now she felt hollow and driven and restless. She wanted to talk to him. Just pick up the phone.

Cut met saucer with a musical jar as she set both on her marble-topped desk. Resisting the first impulse, she lifted the good-luck talisman instead. Laura had pressed the carving into her hands on the morning she'd said goodbye, and Ty's Indian maiden had somehow become the heroine of her story.

'Only you aren't as passive or domesticated as I thought.' Alex traced the smooth-grained features. 'You, Shayna, are much more apt to make the kill than cook the meat. You are brave and strong. You're resourceful, too. A force to be reckoned with.'

There her quiet musings came to a halt, for Alex was well aware she had created Shayna to be everything she was not.

But I've changed! she was stubbornly thinking a moment later. I write every day now. I eat regular meals. I work out. I can sleep without taking pills. I've signed a three-book contract on the strength of one half-finished manuscript, and I'm not going crazy! What more could Jay ask than that?

Unless he had changed too.

Her colour drained. Suppose he didn't want her any more? Suppose his hot blood had cooled, and she went chasing after him, expecting to take up exactly where they'd left off? Wouldn't that be the ultimate humiliation? All these weeks had passed without so much as a call. He must have moved back to Louisville by now; this was September—classes had started. What was she supposed to think? That he was giving her time?

This much time, she reflected grimly, I could have done without!

She glanced longingly at the phone again. What she wouldn't give to hear his voice, fine and low, to see his eyes light with pride. He had been right, completely right! She could tell him that much at least. Maybe invite him over. The hour wasn't all that late, and she was dressed, ready, waiting.

But no—her confidence wavered—that was like flinging her whole body in front of a speeding train. Better to extend a small part of herself, see whether it got shattered.

Sinking into the desk chair, she rested her head in both hands and tried to think rationally about the situation. Right from the start, she'd viewed this book as a gamble—her one shot at proving Alex Stevens for a winner, a survivor, *a girl who knew what she wanted and how to get it*. Telling Jay was supposed to be the culmination of her dream—an event full of joy and shared triumph! She had not foreseen the effect of time. She had not expected to feel *uncertain*.

Alex agonised at length and finally settled on a sample chapter of her manuscript with a careful note inviting Jay to collaborate. The setting had to be perfect, impeccable, she wrote. She knew no one better suited to the role of historical advisor. Would he be interested? On impulse, she added in postcript form, 'A collection of Ty's poems will be published in early December. I only wish he could see it happen. Maybe he can!' She sealed the package quickly, before her heart could tell him more. Then there was nothing to do but wait.

Alex had long since given up waiting when she saw Jay again.

The release of Ty's collection had been timed to coincide with holiday gift-shopping, and on that bitingly cold day the city's largest bookshop had scheduled Alex to appear on her father's behalf. She stood beside a representative from the American Cancer Society, pale with nerves as she surveyed the crowd that had gathered in spite of snow flurries and a predicted winter storm. Why had she ever agreed to this? She had no idea what to say to these people. She felt sick.

By the time she'd shaken a few hands her confidence had revived. The questions mostly concerned Ty and how he'd lived—the kind of man he had been. 'Sad, isn't it?' an elderly lady voiced the general sentiment. 'They say the great artists are never discovered until they're gone.' Holding Alex's hand between both her thin, fragile ones, she added kindly, 'But what a nice thing to do, dear, giving all the money to charity. Is that how he died, then? Cancer?'

Alex nodded wordlessly and tried to smile. When the woman had pressed her hand and moved on she found herself staring at a shirt button, which led up to a taut brown throat, to an attractive beard, and finally to a pair of gravely smiling eyes. *Jay.*

Shock flared undisguised across her features. She actually rocked back on her heels, then froze, praying he hadn't noticed. He looked achingly familiar in jeans and a leather bomber jacket, lean and tall and handsome. His dark eyes roamed her face at length. 'Is this what you set out to do, Alex? Make Ty a folk hero?'

She surreptitiously gripped the table behind her, but kept her tone cool and proud, 'Why not? The critics adore him.'

'So I've heard.' Jay took a copy from the display stand and examined its cover photo: one perfect white dogwood branch against a backdrop of dense green. The motif was repeated throughout the shop, on give-away bookmarks, free-standing signs, rows of banners hanging over their heads. Jay's eyes came back to Alex. *'When The Dogwoods Bloom,'* he quoted softly, like a challenge. 'Appropriate title.'

'Yes, isn't it?' She held his gaze, hurting, her stomach tied up in knots. Had he any idea how much she'd missed him? How many times she'd pictured a scene like this? An accidental meeting?

Seconds ticked away. 'Do you mind, fellow?' prompted a rude voice from several positions back. 'We're all waiting here! Move along and give somebody else a chance.'

Alex could have wept with frustration as Jay grimly surveyed the line. Not yet! she was thinking. Don't go. He turned back to her, eyes dark, face taut. 'How long do you have to be here?' She cast a helpless glance towards the crowd, and his mouth firmed with resignation. 'It doesn't matter. I'll wait.'

Somehow she kept her composure, talking and answering questions with an outward calm, while Jay—

Jay, who had successfully avoided her for the better part of seven months—sat on a bench outside the bookshop with a volume of Ty's poems open across his knee.

Indignation told Alex to ignore him, anticipation bade her to look. Resisting either extreme, she sent furtive glances from beneath her lashes. She couldn't *handle* this. She couldn't.

During a brief lull in the crowd she lifted her head and found Jay's book closed, his brooding stare centred on her. The eye contact sizzled, and she flinched in shock. For an incredible moment she had seen not Jay, but Tangar, the noble savage who stalked her book! His body radiated the same tense strength, the dark and dangerous male beauty; Shayna would have fought to the death for him. Alex felt as if she ought to run!

By the time her duty was discharged she had worked herself into a state of nerves, pride, and righteous anger. Ty's book was available throughout the city, if that was Jay's point, so why come here and upset the delicate balance she had achieved? Why taunt her after rejecting the olive branch of her manuscript? 'Sorry, Alex,' he'd penned, 'but I'm swamped with work right now, and after reading this I can see you have everything under control.'

That's right! Alex resolved. So what could he possibly do to her now?

Exchanging thanks with both the bookshop owner and the charity rep, she shrugged into her wool cape and walked briskly towards the mall entrance. Jay immediately stood, an intensity of expression gripping his lean face. He took a step towards her, and she fought down the crazy impulse to break into flight, thinking *plenty*. He could do plenty.

She stopped before him, looking stylishly elegant in her grey wool cape and flowing challis dress. Her wheat-fair hair was drawn into a classic French braid, her make-up understated but impeccable. She wore the image like armour, for beneath it her heart was jelly, her legs soup. Eyes impassive, she said in a low tone, 'Don't touch me.'

Jay's hand dropped. But his gaze moved over her, more devastating than any tactile contact. 'You've changed.'

'If these past months have proved anything,' she came back, 'then I hope it's that. Yes, I've changed,' she stressed. 'I'm a whole person again.'

What a pitiful lie that was! True, Alex had discovered an incomparable source of satisfaction in her work. She'd survived long lonely hours at the library researching her book, and longer hours at home writing it. She'd found an agent, and negotiated a contract. She'd spent a couple of fun evenings with friends, she'd put her parents' home on the market, she'd got her life back into shape. From her confused past she'd drawn a heritage of colour and inspiration. She'd even shared Thanksgiving dinner with Uncle Stuart and the cousins—all without the benefit of Jay McGee's bracing presence. But there was still an emptiness in her heart. Without him, she would never be whole.

She did not, however, confess to that knowledge, and after a moment he said, 'Then you shouldn't mind talking to me—for old times' sake.' Alex hesitated and he stepped closer, his eyes like dark molten gold. 'I've missed you, honey.'

'Don't call me honey,' she softly scorned. 'And don't talk about missing me, because I find that a little hard to believe. You've been avoiding me since when...last May? And you've just realised you miss me?'

'I've missed you with every *breath*.'

'You know, Jay,' she coolly met his eyes, 'you never used to hand me these lines.'

'Are you so sure it *is* a line?' When she failed to respond he added in a taut voice, 'I thought we had a deal.

You were going to set your life straight and make me a part of it again.'

'That's right.' Alex paled. 'Then you changed your mind.'

A muscle tensed in his jaw, just above the line of his beard, and she fought down an insane urge to smooth it. 'No,' he insisted. 'I was waiting for a sign from you. Some encouragement.'

'Really?' She touched her tongue to dry lips. 'And what would you call my note?'

'Neutral. Impersonal. Confusing. I didn't know what to make of it. Either you'd offered me the collaboration as some kind of consolation prize, or you'd given me an extremely cautious opening. I couldn't decide which.'

'And it never occurred to you to *ask*?'

The moment stretched into a small eternity, his gaze searching, unwavering. He held out a hand, palm up. 'I'm asking now, Alex.'

Her eyes left his hand, locked on to his face. They were blue-grey, icy-hot. She wanted to kick him! She wanted to hug him! 'After all these weeks—after you let me imagine...' She couldn't seem to complete a sentence. Her stomach was doing somersaults. Her lungs refused to draw air. 'Do you have any idea what you've put me through? I thought we were finished. I thought...' She took a tentative step towards him, then stopped. 'Wait a minute.' She stared at him, swallowed drily. 'Why now, Jay? Why not then?'

He hesitated, and the muscle in his jaw spasmodically tightened. 'Because of your postscript,' he finally said. 'Because of Ty.'

Alex swayed, resenting his infernal honesty, despising her own instincts for making his muttered statement so clear. Why hadn't she seen it before? How could she have blindly ignored such a possibility? 'Oh, I get it now!' Anger and betrayal tinged her pale cheeks. 'You read the postscript and assumed I'd found a way to increase my inheritance. You thought I'd sold Ty's soul, didn't you?'

Jay caught her wrist as if he expected her to flee, which she might have tried anyway had her legs felt strong enough to support her. Huskily he got out, '*Yes*. What else was I supposed to think, Alex? That note read like pure business! A cool brush-off, or at the very least some kind of withdrawal. I thought we were finished, too—I thought you'd finished us. Believing I'd misjudged you was my way of staying sane. Only it didn't work,' he admitted in a hoarse tone. 'I went completely crazy without you.'

A brush-off? her brain echoed back. He'd decided her note was a *brush-off*? At the same time a terrible bitterness was growing inside her. 'That must have been quite a blow to your pride,' she said succinctly, 'wanting a girl you couldn't respect!'

Jay winced, but held her eyes. 'I only learned about the charity through yesterday's paper. Forgive me if I didn't guess your intent. That was quite a gesture.'

'No more so than Ty planting a tree every year for the daughter who didn't know him. The collection is my tribute to him,' she said simply, intensely. 'I wanted the world to see my father the way I've come to see him. But, more than that, I wanted to make the kind of statement he might have made. That the eye can't determine everything about a person. True vision comes from the heart.'

Jay grimaced at her unintentional condemnation. 'I tried to phone you, Alex. Yesterday—between classes. Last night I stopped by your apartment, but you weren't there. The doorman refused to let me wait, so I sat across the street in my car. You didn't come home.'

'I ought to let you believe what you're obviously thinking.' She did not miss the flicker of relief in his eyes. 'I spent the last couple of days at my parents' house,' she flatly relented. 'The estate is being sold next week, and I still needed to go through some things. Seems I've developed a real compulsion for tying up loose ends.' She stopped there; he was watching her too closely.

'I hope you mean that.'

'Yes.' She lifted her chin. 'Why?'

'Because I'm taking you home for the weekend.'

Alex could only stare at him. Her heart seemed to turn in her breast, then icy anger surfaced to blot out the momentary flash of warmth. 'If you think,' she furiously found her voice, 'that after all this time, after all the insulting things you believe about me, I would even consider——!'

'No, I don't,' Jay interrupted grimly. 'Not for a minute.' Holding on to the hand she was trying to extract, he turned it over in his palm. 'I wasn't propositioning you, Alex. It's my mother's birthday, that's all. She wants you to be there.'

That's all, Alex repeated to herself a few hours later. Just a family birthday to show her loyalty to Laura. But, sitting beside Jay in the Blazer, her overnight case in the back seat, her eyes on the snow-coated road, all she could really think about was how the cool detachment she'd tried to impress upon him had been nothing but a front. She still found him as attractive as ever. She still loved the way his body moved, the way his voice reminded her of dark honey, even the way his hands held the steering-wheel.

Seeking a distraction, she commented stiffly, 'Kate was in town last month. She said that Jonah might be moving to Frankfort. Did he?'

'Lock, stock, and son,' Jay confirmed. 'He's resigned his job as sheriff to head the governor's task force on rural law enforcement.' He flung her a sideways smile and her heart caught, shuddered. 'I suppose Kate told you about Christina and Joe's new daughter?'

'Yes.' Alex nodded, her return smile strained. 'She also mentioned Adam's five teeth, and the blue ribbon Meredith's calf won at the state fair.' She heard her tense voice and hated the way it sounded, so flat, so completely uninspired. She really liked Jay's family. She'd exchanged several letters with Laura. She'd even called on occasion. Glancing out of the window, she murmured distractedly, 'I hear you're gaining Paula as a sister-in-law.'

'That's right, Jake finally took the plunge.' Jay flicked on the windscreen wipers, frowning at a sudden maelstrom of white. 'Keep your seatbelt fastened, honey. It's really coming down out there.'

Alex realised that he needed all his concentration just to drive. The rest of the trip passed in relative silence, Jay peering grimly at the road, and she chewing her lip as she gazed out of the window, wondering for the umpteenth time what she'd got herself into.

Her mouth tugged into a reluctant smile as they passed Jake's Garage, for the building and canopy had been cleaned and given a handsome coat of paint. Unless she was mistaken, the blue and burgundy colour scheme bore Paula's touch. The windows sparkled clear and bright, and a new picket fence kept the junked cars out the back from being an eyesore. Betsy, though, was just as muddy as ever, and Alex thought with wry humour that there were some things even a determined woman couldn't change.

Then they started up the mountain, and for no good reason she began to feel tense. They hadn't even talked about sleeping arrangements—not that she had anything to worry about, because Jay automatically passed his own cabin and turned up the drive to Alex's little house. Shivering, and praying that she could still build a fire, she turned to lift her case from the back seat.

Covering her hand with his own, Jay insisted hoarsely, 'Leave it.' Alex stared at his lean fingers and wet her mouth. He had gone oddly still when she lifted her head. A pulse beat visibly in his temple. Tension spun out between them, looping back like a weighted net. 'All your dogwoods are pink, Alex. Why did you choose white for the book?'

His unexpected question evoked a completely candid response. 'Because Ty had the purest heart I've ever known.' A tightness gripped her chest... a strangely *comfortable* tightness, not unlike some fleeting embrace. 'Just look at those trees.' Eyes soft now, luminous, she surveyed the homestead. 'One way or another, he was determined to give me some roots!'

Jay sent a slow, unsmiling glance across the yard. 'Sometimes a gesture is clearer than words, Alex. Sometimes it's a statement so clean, so unmistakable, that there are no questions left.' He sounded grave, intense, as if something of great significance was riding on this moment. 'Of all the things Ty taught me, that's the one thing I'm pinning my hopes on right now.'

He got out of the truck and reached to help her down. Feet crunching on new snow, heart beating erratically, Alex followed. She surveyed Ty's stair-step trees with their white-covered branches, remembering how gorgeous they'd looked in full bloom. Then she stopped abruptly, and her throat closed. Because there, where it had not been last spring, was a young dogwood with the identification tag still attached, a bare earth mound about its roots.

Alex, who had not really cried in months and had even congratulated herself on finally developing a bit of steel, felt emotional tears welling in her eyes, and could do nothing about them. She bent to slide a finger along one of the ice-coated branches, half sobbing. 'But it's so tiny, Jay, and the air is freezing! What if it doesn't survive?' Impulsively and ridiculously she stripped off her cape and draped it over the baby tree.

Jay laughed softly and immediately surrounded her with the warmth of his own coat and his arms. 'That little dogwood is a lot sturdier than you are.' Then he felt the quivers that ran through her slight body. 'Don't cry, sweetheart. But does the fact that you *are* crying mean you've forgiven me...at least a little?'

With her face pressed against his chest she sobbed, 'I could be persuaded.'

'And could you also be persuaded to marry me?' he came back. 'Because, if not, then I'm afraid I'll have to borrow my next move from someone not nearly so subtle as your father.'

Alex pulled away a bit, blinking wet lashes and fighting the urge to lose herself in his crinkling eyes. 'Thank you for my birthday tree,' she whispered. 'It was a lovely gesture, and I'll cherish it, but a few words might not go amiss just now. I've been so sure you didn't want me.'

'*Want* you?' Jay softly and fiercely devoured her mouth, muttering huskily between kisses, 'Alex, I *ached* for you. You don't know how many times I wanted to beat down your door!'

'Really?' A shudder racked her, half delight, half pain. 'Why didn't you?'

'Because the first move had to be yours.' He dipped a kiss into her dimple, groaning, 'And what a move it was! That note really threw me, sweetheart. I imagined all kinds of grim possibilities. Such as, you didn't need me any more.' He rubbed his beard against her jaw. 'Such as, you'd rediscovered your own world and decided I had no place in it.' He nipped the corner of her mouth. 'Such as, you'd changed.' Cupping her face in both hands, he stared deep into her eyes. 'I should have remembered *your* pure heart. From now on, that's one of life's constants.'

'Brilliant touch, Professor.' Brushing snowflakes from his beard, Alex gave him a watery smile. 'Anything else?'

'A couple of things.' He grinned tenderly and lowered his head. 'I love you. I adore you. I'm wild about you.'

Later, back at Jay's cabin, Alex lay comfortably cradled on his lap while he told her again—with remarkably few words—how much he'd missed her. When she finally lifted her head the elegant French braid had been charmingly dishevelled, her shoes lost in the sofa cushions, and any remaining doubts completely overruled. She stared dazedly into the fire, then glanced around the familiar room. 'Your artefacts!' Her blue-grey eyes widened. 'Where are they?'

'On permanent loan to the university.' Jay kissed the top of her head. 'I could hardly justify keeping them here—not after that mini-museum crack.'

'See? And you didn't believe I could make a difference.'

'I was wrong.' With a grave smile and obvious satisfaction he predicted, 'Your book is going to make a lot of people re-think their views, Alex. I can't imagine any greater testimony to the spirit of our ancestors. You made them *breathe*. I'm proud of you.'

'Thanks.' She smiled back tremulously and laid a hand along his lean cheek. 'But, as much as I love you and your compliments, I suppose we should think about Laura. When is her party?'

For a moment Jay looked nonplussed. Then he shrugged and said vaguely, 'Some time in February. I'll have to let you know.'

Eyes round, incredulous, Alex gaped at him. She struggled up, ignoring a wince as her elbow glanced off his ribs. 'Do you mean to say,' she breathed, 'that you *lied* to me?'

'How else was I going to get you here?' He exaggeratedly rubbed his side. 'I told you I wouldn't fight fair.'

'But I thought you were bluffing!' Alex knew she should be cross with him. Instead she found herself sighing and settling close again, pressing her blonde head to his chest. For a long time she listened to the heavy thud of his heart, to the rushing in-and-out of blood that seemed to echo a primitive chant. Power. Oneness. Trust. She sensed his body gathering strength, trading tenderness for taut passion. Then he rose to carry her towards the stairs, and she wavered between agonised conscience and delight. This was such an un-gentlemanly thing to do; she felt she ought to stop him. '*Jay.*' But her voice carried more shock than resolve, and he knew it.

'I thought you were going to be my wife?'

'Yes, I am, but——'

'Close enough,' he declared in a low drawl. 'You've known right from the start, Alex, I'm not a hundred per cent. And, besides,' he added wickedly with another kiss, 'who did you think I had in mind when I mentioned borrowing my next move? Tangar, honey. Blame yourself and that book of yours, but I think the guy was on to something.'

Holiday Romance

Make your holiday extra special with four new Romances from Mills & Boon.

PLANTATION SUMMER
Angela Devine

VENDETTA BRIDE
Rebecca King

TREACHEROUS PATH
Joanna Neil

A HEART DIVIDED
Lee Stafford

Four Romances by four popular authors have been specially chosen for this exciting gift selection.

What could be easier to pack for your holiday!

Published: 12th June 1992   Price: £6.80

*Available from Boots, Martins, John Menzies, W.H. Smith, most supermarkets and other paperback stockists.
Also available from Mills & Boon Reader Service, PO Box 236, Thornton Road, Croydon, Surrey CR9 3RU.*

PENNY JORDAN

A COLLECTION

From the bestselling author of *Power Play*, *Silver* and *The Hidden Years* comes a special collection of three early novels, beautifully presented in one volume.

Featuring:

SHADOW MARRIAGE
MAN-HATER
PASSIONATE PROTECTION

Available from May 1992   Priced £4.99

Available from Boots, Martins, John Menzies, W.H. Smith, most supermarkets and other paperback stockists.
Also available from Mills & Boon Reader Service, PO Box 236, Thornton Road, Croydon, Surrey CR9 3RU.

W●RLDWIDE

Accept 4 FREE Romances and 2 FREE gifts

FROM READER SERVICE

An irresistible invitation from Mills & Boon Reader Service. Please accept our offer of 4 free Romances, a CUDDLY TEDDY and a special MYSTERY GIFT... Then, if you choose, go on to enjoy 6 captivating Romances every month for just £1.70 each, postage and packing free. Plus our FREE Newsletter with author news, competitions and much more.

**Send the coupon below to:
Reader Service, FREEPOST,
PO Box 236, Croydon,
Surrey CR9 9EL.**

NO STAMP REQUIRED

Yes! Please rush me 4 Free Romances and 2 free gifts!
Please also reserve me a Reader Service Subscription. If I decide to subscribe I can look forward to receiving 6 brand new Romances each month for just £10.20, post and packing free.
If I choose not to subscribe I shall write to you within 10 days - I can keep the books and gifts whatever I decide. I may cancel or suspend my subscription at any time. I am over 18 years of age.

Ms/Mrs/Miss/Mr ————————————————————————— EP30R

Address ————————————————————————————————

————————————————————————————————————

Postcode——————————Signature ———————————

Offer expires 31st May 1993. The right is reserved to refuse an application and change the terms of this offer. Readers overseas and in Eire please send for details.
Southern Africa write to Book Services International Ltd, P.O. Box 42654, Craighall, Transvaal 2024.
You may be mailed with offers from other reputable companies as a result of this application. If you would prefer not to share in this opportunity, please tick box ☐

Next Month's Romances

Each month you can choose from a world of variety in romance with Mills & Boon. Below are the new titles to look out for next month, why not ask either Mills & Boon Reader Service or your Newsagent to reserve you a copy of the titles you want to buy — just tick the titles you would like to order and either post to Reader Service or take it to any Newsagent and ask them to order your books.

Please save me the following titles:	Please tick	√
STORMFIRE	Helen Bianchin	
LAW OF ATTRACTION	Penny Jordan	
DANGEROUS SANCTUARY	Anne Mather	
ROMANTIC ENCOUNTER	Betty Neels	
A DARING PROPOSITION	Miranda Lee	
NO PROVOCATION	Sophie Weston	
LAST OF THE GREAT FRENCH LOVERS	Sarah Holland	
CAVE OF FIRE	Rebecca King	
NO MISTRESS BUT LOVE	Kate Proctor	
INTRIGUE	Margaret Mayo	
ONE LOVE FOREVER	Barbara McMahon	
DOUBLE FIRE	Mary Lyons	
STONE ANGEL	Helen Brooks	
THE ORCHARD KING	Miriam Macgregor	
LAW OF THE CIRCLE	Rosalie Ash	
THE HOUSE ON CHARTRES STREET	Rosemary Hammond	

If you would like to order these books from Mills & Boon Reader Service please send £1.70 per title to: Mills & Boon Reader Service, P.O. Box 236, Croydon, Surrey, CR9 3RU and quote your Subscriber No:..(If applicable) and complete the name and address details below. Alternatively, these books are available from many local Newsagents including W.H.Smith, J.Menzies, Martins and other paperback stockists from 6th July 1992.

Name:..
Address:..
....Post Code:.....................

To Retailer: If you would like to stock M&B books please contact your regular book/magazine wholesaler for details.

You may be mailed with offers from other reputable companies as a result of this application. If you would rather not take advantage of these opportunities please tick box ☐